"Do you even know how many cops are in the station right now, waiting to nab us?" I whispered.

Narrowing her eyes, Abby scanned the concourse. "Whoa. Okay, head for the west exit. It's closest. Believe me, I scoped it out. I had all kinds of maps and diagrams and I used MapQuest and —"

"Just come on," I said, and we hurried down the platform.

Some army, huh?

A fat boy, his dead brother, and a chatty girl with a cane.

We didn't stand a chance.

THE RED HOUSE

Look for these titles in
THE HAUNTING OF DEREK STONE series:

THE RED HOUSE

⊰ TONY ABBOTT ⊱

SCHOLASTIC INC.

NEW YORK   TORONTO   LONDON   AUCKLAND   SYDNEY
MEXICO CITY   NEW DELHI   HONG KONG   BUENOS AIRES

ISBN-13: 978-0-545-03431-9
ISBN-10: 0-545-03431-0

12 11 10 9 8 7 6 5 4 3 2 1   9 10 11 12 13 14/0

Printed in the U.S.A.   40

First printing, June 2009

To Those Who Cannot Leave

⊲ CONTENTS ⊳

THE RED HOUSE

◄| ONE |►

Mystery Boy

H*e died.*

Two words, and my dumb little life changed forever.

Six letters, and the world I believed in vanished into nothing, like fog in the wind.

"I won't believe it!" I cried, falling to my knees. "I won't!"

"You must believe it," was the stone-cold reply.

As sunny and warm as the day began, night dropped hard and fast like the lid of a coffin.

The horror of it made me sick. I didn't want to go on. I *couldn't* go on.

I mean, how would *you* feel if someone told you —

Wait.

You couldn't possibly know how you'd feel unless you understood — really understood — what I'm talking about.

So let me wipe the blood from my forehead and go back nine hours to this morning.

I'll tell you everything that happened from that moment to now. You need to know where we came from to understand where we are now.

We? Right. Let me start there.

My name is Derek Stone. I'm fourteen, fat, smarter than most people I know, and on the run. Nine hours ago, my older brother, Ronny, and I were holed up in a filthy room in a fleabag hotel on the outskirts of Baton Rouge, Louisiana. We'd been there since four a.m. the night before.

It was 11:21 a.m. when I opened my eyes. The blinds were down, but sunlight sliced through them like a hot knife through butter. The air was a white haze. The room was an oven.

"How'd you pick this dump, anyway?" I asked Ronny, rolling off the mattress and onto my feet. "I feel horrible."

"You look horrible," Ronny snorted from the bathroom sink. "Being on the run means being on a budget. Our money's almost out."

I flipped open my cell. Black screen. Dead battery. "I wish I could charge this thing," I said. "In case Abby calls again."

Abby Donner. My phone had died last night in the middle of a call from her.

More about her later.

"Toss that thing," said Ronny. "The cops can trace it, right? Besides, Abby's train comes in half an hour. Get dressed."

I pulled on my pants and shirt and muscled Ronny out of the bathroom. I held my breath as he passed.

Why did I hold my breath? Because Ronny is decaying.

"Decaying?" you say. "The dude's only nineteen. How could he be decaying? Only corpses do that, right?"

Right. Only corpses.

Man, I'm tired of telling this story. But you need to hear it. Your life depends on it, though you may not know it yet. So listen up, and bear with me. There's a lot to tell, and not much time.

A few weeks ago Ronny, my father, and I were in a bad train wreck. Maybe you heard about it. Big news. The old bridge over Bordelon Gap collapsed. Our train fell into the ravine. Ronny was one of nine passengers killed.

Then he came back.

Came back?

Trust me, that's the easy part.

"We're out of here," Ronny said. He pulled me into the hotel hallway with all my worldly possessions:

twenty-something dollars, twenty pounds of extra fat, a headache, and a case of the shakes.

"Let's skedaddle," he added.

Skedaddle? That's exactly what I'm talking about.

Ronny came back from the train wreck — at least, his body did. Inside him was the soul of a young man named Virgil Black. Virgil died in an almost identical train crash at the same place back in 1938. Because the two accidents were so alike, and because the curtain that separates the worlds of the living and the dead has been torn — I call it the Rift — souls in the afterlife were able to enter the crash victims at the moment they died.

"*Enter* the crash victims?" you say.

Yep. Reanimate them.

Like, "Hello! We're back!"

It's the old body, but a different soul. I call this grotesque process of soul-switching *translation*.

Another one of the train wreck victims was my father. He was missing for weeks, presumed dead, since all they could find of him was his hand. But then he turned up alive and *un*translated . . . I think.

The souls who came back at the crash site are a pack of notorious convicts, led by a murderous thug named Erskine Cane. I'd learned pretty quickly that these dark souls are only the advance troops of a massive dead-guy army called the Legion.

The Legion.

The word makes me nauseous.

"Come on," Ronny said, slinging his small bag into the trunk of a beat-up green Subaru that belonged to his ex-girlfriend, Samantha. It had looked much nicer before we'd borrowed it. "Clock's ticking."

I slid into the passenger seat.

According to Ronny — or Virgil — for centuries, the evil souls of the Legion have been warring against good souls in the afterlife. And they're winning. Once they discovered the Rift, they began translating into dead bodies and bringing their war up here.

Why?

To take over.

Since Virgil is a soldier on the good side, he knows that evil souls are angry, vindictive. They want revenge on the good, on the living, on everyone better off than them. Ronny told me that the afterlife of evil people is like perpetual torture. It's horrible. So the dark souls want out. They want to come back here.

No matter what it means for the living.

In addition to Cane, who returned in the body of a giant, muscle-bound soldier, there was a strong wiry dude with a nervous tic who I call Twitchy. Another convict returned in the body of the train conductor, who lost an arm in the accident. There's also an amazingly tough gray-haired old man. He beat me up once. I definitely don't like him.

There are three or four others, too.

Or there were, until last night.

Last night, the Legion picked up another fifty or so evil souls in a place called Bayou Malpierre. Those souls — in the bodies of bayou tourists — are led by a creepy little blind boy named Waldo Fouks. The soul inside Waldo's body is actually the leader of a murderous band of riverboat smugglers.

Nice, right?

Waldo was totally weird. But he did tell me I was "special." He called me "mystery boy."

I hope that goes in my permanent record.

"I don't like this," Ronny said. He slowed the car and pulled over to the curb to let four police cruisers tear past us.

"You don't think they know about us, do you?" I said.

"Maybe," he said quietly. "Maybe Uncle Carl told them to look for us." The police cars roared up the street and away. After a minute, Ronny pulled back into traffic.

My father's brother Carl had stayed with me in New Orleans after the train crash. He was there when Ronny came back, but he didn't know the whole story. He just thought Ronny was out of sorts, traumatized. He couldn't have imagined the truth. Uncle Carl was out of town when Erskine Cane burned down our house in the French Quarter.

Ronny and I had been hiding out ever since. It was only a matter of time before the cops got involved, really. With a mass translation in the bayou, with Dad leading the cops on a wild-goose chase so we could get away, with people "dying" and then mysteriously "coming back," the cops would soon be all over our war with the dead.

The war, I called it.

Simple but effective.

"I'll park a few blocks from the station, just to be safe," Ronny said. Then he snorted. "Safe? Some joke, huh?"

Neither one of us was laughing.

But it gets worse.

Over the last few days, I've learned that the Legion is searching for someone called the First — the first one translated. He's here, in the world of the living. From what I'm getting, the First is the Legion's ultimate leader here. He's even worse than giant Cane or creepy Waldo. Great.

Ronny paused at a light, searching right and left for a good parking spot. More police cars roared up behind us, lights flashing, but no sirens. Ronny grumbled and turned down a side street.

So how do I know about the First?

Because everyone keeps telling me, that's how.

To begin with, Abby Donner — the girl we were going to meet at the train station — was in a coma after the crash. She says that while she was in the coma, her mother, Madeline Donner, came to her and told her about the Legion. And Abby remembers it. What Abby doesn't know is that her mom's body is now inhabited by the soul of Erskine Cane's crazy wife. And, like Ronny, she's decaying, too. Pretty bad, huh?

I've seen Cane's wife a few times already, and each time she told me the same thing.

"The First . . ." she said. *"The First . . ."*

As if she was trying to warn me or something.

I guess it makes sense that anyone related to Abby wouldn't be all bad.

Oh. Something else happened in Bayou Malpierre, too. Ten years ago, when I was four, I nearly drowned there. I was under that murky gray water for a long time. And while I was almost drowning, I apparently *saw* the First. At least that's what my dad told me.

Of course, I have no memory of what really happened in the bayou ten years ago. But did that stop the dead from haunting me? Not so much.

You also have to know that Waldo Fouks's father, Bonton, was actually a decent guy, who died defending Ronny and me from his creepy son. He didn't know who Waldo really was until then. Just before he died, Bonton gave me a photograph of an old red house. He'd found it on me when I was little, after I was saved from drowning, and he kept it hidden for ten years. When I saw the picture again, I knew that house right away. I just didn't know how. Or why. Call me crazy, but I also knew that the rusty iron key I had found would open something in the red house.

Abby had called the night before to tell me that she had discovered the location of the mysterious red house. So Ronny and I hightailed it to Baton Rouge to meet her. We had to get to the red house — wherever it was — before the Legion did.

Time was running out. They'd left the bayou in search of the red house themselves, almost as if someone had commanded them to.

The First?

That's what I'm thinking. But what do I know?

All I knew for sure was that we had to find that red house, figure out what the key opened, and hope that it would help us stop the Legion before they took over the world.

Not much. Just that.

"Here we are." Ronny stopped the Subaru at a curb three and a half blocks from the train station. "Hurry it up, Tubs."

There's love for you. One of the weirdest things about Ronny is that even though he's Virgil Black now — a farm boy from upstate, in Shongaloo — there are still bits of Ronny in him. An occasional look. A phrase. A gesture. Something.

So I still call him Ronny.

Virgil doesn't seem to mind.

I followed him along the sidewalk. It was 11:51 a.m. Our day had begun.

⊰ TWO ⊱

Abby Donner

Abby's train was due at noon, and it was four minutes to twelve by the time we arrived in the main concourse of the train station.

I was about to tell Ronny how being anywhere near trains made me sick to my stomach, but then I saw the blazer.

Navy blue, shiny, saggy in the shoulders, with a bulge under the left arm. And then another blazer just like it, and another, and another. Between and above the baggy shoulders were thick necks, sweaty foreheads, and darting eyes.

"Police?" I said. "Federal agents?"

Ronny glanced furiously from face to face as the men moved quickly into every corner of the large room. "This is bad. If they bring us in, they won't believe a word we say, and the Legion will keep growing until it's too late. Slip into the shadows. If I lose you, I'll meet you on the street behind the building. Keep out of sight. We may have to start running."

Running? That loosened something in my head, and strange words echoed from my memory.

Children of light, lost, so lost, running in darkness . . .

I shivered to hear those words in my mind. Like other words I'd "heard" since the accident, I had no clue what these meant. But they sure seemed to be about Ronny and me.

. . . lost, so lost, running in darkness . . .

And maybe Abby, too.

Ronny pulled me out of the main room toward platform thirteen. We ducked into a bagel shop when a couple of guys in blazers passed.

"Uh-oh, Ronny," I whispered. "Look up there."

A flat-screen TV behind the counter showed grainy nighttime footage of water rushing through a big swamp.

Bayou Malpierre. I knew it.

My chest buzzed when a TV voice-over began describing the incident. I couldn't hear everything, but I could hear enough. "Flash flood . . . broken lock . . . crested levees . . . bayou tour boats . . . startling rescue . . ." The video then showed a car hidden among the bayou overgrowth.

Our green Subaru.

"That's it," Ronny said. "They know about the car, and they're closing in. There's her train."

The train from New Orleans squealed to a stop, and right away the platform was flooded with passengers. We waited in the bagel shop, scanning the crowd. Almost the last person to leave the train was a girl with long brown hair tied in a loose ponytail. Abby Donner. She wore blue shorts and a green T-shirt, and had a big handbag slung over her shoulder.

Abby had broken her ankle in the train wreck a month ago, but when she walked down the platform, I saw that her ankle cast was gone. She was using a wooden cane.

"I'm going," I said.

Ronny grabbed my arm. "Wait for her to come a little closer —"

"I'm going." I pushed out of the shop and walked quickly to the platform, head down, hoping no one would notice me.

Abby's eyes were tired, and her face looked pale, but she managed a smile when she spotted me. "Hey, Derek."

"We can't be here," I whispered, taking her arm.

"Hello to you, too," she said, stopping. "Do you even know how much guts it took for me to get on a train again, or what I went through to find that weird old house for you?"

"Do you even know how many cops are in the station right now, waiting to nab us?" I whispered.

Her face changed. Narrowing her eyes, she scanned the concourse. "Whoa. Okay, head for the west exit. It's closest. Believe me, I scoped it out. I had all kinds of maps and diagrams and I used MapQuest and —"

"Just come on," I said, and we hurried down the platform.

Some army, huh?

A fat boy, his dead brother, and a chatty girl with a cane.

We didn't stand a chance.

All at once, someone in a blue blazer bolted across the concourse toward our platform. A shrill whistle sounded, a man yelled, and agents fanned out across the big room. I glanced over at the bagel shop. Ronny was gone.

"Let's get out of here!" I hissed. Abby and I took the first set of stairs we saw.

"Just so you know, I don't like stairs," she said.

But there was no choice — she half-jumped down as quickly as she could. We made our way to street level and hurried down a tunnel, nearly colliding with Ronny, who joined us from a connecting tunnel.

Together, the three of us hustled through two or three more passages and out a service exit.

"Where's the car?" asked Abby, once we reached the sidewalk.

Before Ronny or I could answer, three police cars tore down the street toward the green Subaru.

"How about we walk?" I said.

"And let's make it fast," Ronny added, looking both ways and pushing through the gathering crowd to the curb.

We darted out into the street between lights and among cars. Horns blared. Drivers shouted. We didn't care.

More police cars raced down the street, but we were already gone.

◄⊪ THREE ⊪►

The Memorial

We hustled through the hot streets on foot, first with Ronny in the lead, then Abby. I knew she was in pain, hobbling on her healing ankle, but she said nothing except "Right," "Left," and "Straight ahead."

"Where are you taking us?" Ronny panted.

"School," she said.

"What?"

But Abby just hurried on.

Ronny looked back over his shoulder constantly. The gray patch on his neck was bigger than I remembered from last night. Darker, too.

A half hour later, we huffed and puffed our way through the tall cast-iron gates of Louisiana State University.

"School, huh? Why are we here?" Ronny asked as we entered a broad avenue lined with poplar trees.

"The war memorial," Abby replied simply.

"Oh, yeah? Which war?" Ronny grumbled with a scowl. He didn't sound as if he really expected an answer.

We took several more twists and turns, and before long arrived at a structure that looked like a bank with a clock tower sprouting out of the top like a mission steeple.

"This war memorial was built to commemorate the Louisianans lost in the First World War," Abby said. "In the basement is what's left of something called the Dixie Museum. It has tons of documents and photographs and stuff relating to the Civil War in Louisiana."

"And?" said Ronny.

"And," Abby continued, "I'm pretty sure it's got information about your red house."

My heart thumped as I pulled the old photograph from my pocket. "Really, you found this place?"

"Sort of," she said. "You'll see. Come on."

Abby and I started up the memorial steps, but Ronny was frozen, staring at a little old car in the nearby parking lot. A student in a baseball cap had just gotten out of it and was now hustling past us, into the memorial.

I looked at Ronny. "What's the big deal?"

"He left his keys in the car," Ronny said quietly.

I snorted a laugh. "Who'd want to steal that thing, anyway?"

"Yeah, who?" Ronny snickered. Then he turned to follow Abby up the stairs and inside.

After passing the security checkpoint, we headed for a bank of elevators. Abby pressed the down button.

"Uh . . . I don't like being cooped up in iron boxes," Ronny mumbled, his eyes darting everywhere. "I'll take the stairs."

Ping! The doors opened. The elevator was empty.

"We'll meet you one floor down," Abby told Ronny.

"Yeah, yeah," he said. "I know where basements are."

He slunk off down a hallway, and the elevator doors closed on me and Abby.

"He's not doing so well, is he?" she asked, turning to face me.

I shook my head. Ronny's finger was black with rot where he had cut it trying to shave, and the tip was gone. The gray patch on his neck was getting bigger by the day. And those were just the places I could see. I knew the rotting smell made him avoid close quarters, like the elevator. It was an ugly thought, but I wondered how long Ronny would be around before he decayed completely.

Of course, the big question was why Ronny was decaying so quickly in the first place — even though the Legion wasn't. I had theories. It seemed to have something to do with *where* they died. Ronny died on the rocks in the ravine, on land. So did Madeline Donner, who also seemed to be decaying. But those who died in the water hadn't started to decay.

Not yet, at least.

Whoosh. The elevator doors slid open. It was cooler in the basement, and the air smelled like musty old paper.

When Ronny joined us, we walked through two rooms of the little museum before slowing in a third.

"I had almost nothing to go on," Abby said. "You have an old photograph of a red plantation house. My mother told me the dead are searching for a red house, too. But I knew there must be a thousand red houses in dozens of parishes all over the state. So, since your photo is so old, I went way back in the past."

"What did you find?" I asked.

Abby led me to a glass display case marked "Pre-War Plantations Lost and Found." She tapped the glass over one of the photographs there. "Is this it?"

I gasped.

It was the same house in the photograph that Bonton had given me. The angle was different, and the house had changed over the years, but I recognized it instantly. Its walls were tinged red, its roof sagged, two of the monumental columns were cracked and leaning, and the cast-iron fence that showed the same floral design as the iron key was flat on the ground.

Trembling, I focused on the typewritten label next to the photo as Abby read it aloud.

"The house is called Amaranthia — Derek!"

I slumped to the floor and blacked out for a second. When I came to, my head burned and my bad ear buzzed.

Ronny knelt next to me. "Could someone please get some water?"

A female security guard hurried over and helped me into a nearby chair. I sat with my head between my knees to get the blood flowing again.

"It must be the terrible heat," the woman said sympathetically.

It wasn't the heat.

"Amaranthia," I said softly. "Amaranthia."

And words I'd heard somewhere before came to me again.

Within your crimson walls, I was an angel child;

From room to room I floated in your wingless window light . . .

"The house is named after the amaranth flower," Abby said, patting my hand the way they do in old movies when you faint. "It's a big red blossom, almost coral."

I knew all that, of course. How I knew it, I couldn't say. Odd things had been sloshing around in my head ever since the accident — words, names, sounds, voices. And all in the ear in which I'd heard hardly anything since I nearly drowned ten years before.

Completely weird, I know.

"I'm okay," I said, standing and walking slowly back to the display.

Like tumblers falling into place, snippets of knowledge and fact, memories, maybe even dreams, all shuttled across the surface of my mind until they found their proper positions. Something clicked.

"Amaranthia was the ancestral home of the Longtemps family," I said. "My mother — our mother," I said to Ronny, "was a Longtemps. The house is a few miles from Compson, in Coushatta, on the Red River."

Ronny scowled at me. He was Virgil Black now, not Ronny Longtemps Stone.

"The Red River," he said. "What a surprise."

I knew what he meant. Every translation so far had been on or near the Red River or one of its tributaries. The Red River ran hard and fast through Bordelon Gap. Bayou Malpierre was on the Atchafalaya, an offshoot of the Red River. And now we were headed to Coushatta, on its banks.

How I knew where the house was — without even looking at the display — made no sense. A total mystery. But it wasn't the biggest mystery.

I had never been to anyplace called Coushatta. I doubted I'd ever even said the word out loud. But in my mind I saw its grassy green banks sweeping up from the river to a big lawn, and a garden dotted with wild amaranth blossoms as the morning sun hit them after a long rain.

What was that? A painting? A memory? What?

"Amaranthia was built in 1821," said Abby, reading from the exhibit. "It was a plantation at the center of a hundred-square-mile tract of land that spanned both sides of the river."

Leaning over the photograph, with my hands braced on the glass cabinet, I said, "I know all that."

"Why does that not surprise me?" said Abby. "Derek, you are —"

Her cell phone rang. Her face flushed when she saw who was calling. She raised the phone to her ear. "Hi . . . No, I'm fine. Nora, I'm absolutely fine. . . ."

Abby was talking to Grammy Nora, her grandmother, a cool lady who didn't quite believe what Ronny and I had told her about the living dead, but who loved her granddaughter and so had helped us.

"Because I can't get you involved in this . . ." Abby said.

I heard Nora practically screaming on the other end of the line.

"Did you skip out without telling her?" I whispered.

Abby gave me a look. I shut up. "Grammy, I love you. I know, but trust me. My mother came to me. She told me about the house. Trust me. This is important."

The voice on the other end began to speak more softly.

"I know," Abby went on. "And I will. Look, these guys are all right. They'll take care of me." She pulled the phone away from her face and whispered, "You'd *better* take care of me!" Then back in the phone: "I know. I will absolutely call you tonight. Baton Rouge. Right. I love you, too."

Listening made me sad. Sad for Nora, who didn't know the half of it. Sad for Abby, who would soon figure out her mother was one of the translated dead. Sad for Ronny, who was on the wrong side of being dead. And sure, I was sad for me, too. Why not? I was smack in the middle of this horror.

"The Longtempses were a powerful family, but the Civil War changed everything," Abby read from the display. "The family lost its land acre by acre. Only a few fields and the shell of the house remain today."

I didn't say, "I know" — but I did. I knew everything she said. What place in my mind held all this weird information? What kind of freak was I?

"Amaranthia was known as the 'Jewel of Coushatta,'" I said randomly.

"It's hours from here," Ronny added.

Did my mother know about her family's house? Was she the one who first told me about it so that I remembered it? I hadn't seen her for ten years. All I could recall was standing next to her in the cemetery before she left my life forever.

"The house is now derelict, inaccessible from modern roads," Abby read.

I pulled the old key from my pocket. It was rusted iron but not large, so I knew it wasn't a house or gate key. I instinctively knew it belonged to something in the house. The floral pattern inside the key's oval grip was the same amaranth as on the fence, the doors, everything. "Maybe it opens a chest, or a closet door," I murmured.

"Or a box or a desk drawer," said Abby.

"Okay, look," Ronny spat, pacing the room like a caged tiger. "First of all, keep your voices down. And second, the Legion saw you with the key in the bayou, Derek. They'll know about the house. We don't have time for guessing games. We have to find what the key opens, and we have to do it now."

"Maybe they don't know where the house is," Abby whispered.

"They know," said Ronny sharply, his eyes shooting around the room. He moved toward the door. "They aren't people, remember. They're the Legion. Centuries of warring in the afterlife have made them different from you and . . ."

Ronny trailed off. I knew why. He was about to say, "Different from you and me." But that wasn't true. He was like them. A dead soul, back again.

"Ronny, listen," I started, but a sharp, lemony smell wafted into the room and distracted me. I turned to Abby. "Are you wearing perfume?"

"What?" she asked.

Suddenly, the air thumped, and shards of wood and glass sprayed across the room. I was thrown to the floor. Alarms went off. Sprinklers spurted. Abby screamed. Ronny yelled.

Then came a second blast. More glass flying — and the sound of running feet.

⊰ FOUR ⊱

Rest Stop

Was it seconds? Minutes? Longer? I couldn't tell you.

Sirens whooped in my good ear. Sprinklers spurted, and the water mixed with the dust in the air, muddying the floor. The security guard scrambled to her feet and called for help on her walkie-talkie. "Injuries . . . basement of the memorial . . . Hurry . . ."

I wondered for an instant if she was talking about me. But when I got up, I knew I wasn't hurt badly, even though I'd been thrown across the room. I hoped Abby was all right. I didn't see her anywhere. I knew Ronny would be okay — he'd been halfway out of the room at the time.

"Abby!" I called out.

Then I saw someone, half-visible in the smoke, rolling on the floor. I was afraid it was Abby, but just then Abby rushed toward me out of the dust, waving it from her face as two men in uniform burst into the room. The guard pointed her walkie-talkie at the student in the baseball cap, and they hurried across the room to him, ducking under the sprinklers. The student was clutching his leg and groaning loudly.

"Come on," said Ronny, appearing out of nowhere and grabbing my arm. "We need to go. Now."

We left the room in chaos. Ronny took us up the stairs. It was mayhem in the lobby, too. Everyone was being checked quickly, then evacuated, but we couldn't have that. What would they find if they checked Ronny? A troop of armed security and medical people raced past us. With all the distractions, we were able to sneak by the others and hurry to the parking lot, Abby hobbling quickly on her cane.

Ronny went straight to the little old car he'd spotted earlier. "Get in," he said, climbing into the driver's seat. "That guy won't be needing it anytime soon. We're doing him a favor."

"Wait a second, Ronny —" Abby started.

"Get in!" he commanded.

We did. He started the car. "Full tank. Good thing. We don't have money to spare on gas."

We pulled into the line of cars being rushed off campus.

"Why did that happen?" I asked after a minute. "Who did it?"

Ronny shook his head. "I don't know, but it wasn't much of an explosion."

"Oh, no?" Abby said from the backseat. "That guy looked pretty hurt —"

"I know he was hurt," Ronny said, "but from the glass in the display case. Not shrapnel. Not exploding metal. Not a real bomb. I know about those things. This wasn't the same. This wasn't the Legion."

I knew that Ronny was right. It wasn't the Legion. But it wasn't the explosion that made it clear. It was because there was no water. The Legion was always near water.

Abby and I glanced at each other. I knew we were both thinking the same thing. If not a big bomb, if not to hurt us, then who set it off and why? I remembered the smell of perfume just before the explosion. Why did I bother to notice it in the first place? Did it mean anything?

As more emergency vehicles flew past, Ronny finally tore out of the university campus and onto the street again, heading out of the city.

"There's something else I need to tell you," Abby said hesitantly. She closed her eyes for a second, then opened them. "My mother . . ."

Uh-oh, I thought. "Yeah?"

"She's dead . . . and not dead, isn't she?"

"What?"

I didn't know what to say.

"She's been translated. You're trying to keep it from me, but I'm not stupid. Just stubborn. She died in the train crash, but she's back, isn't she? It's the only thing that makes sense."

Abby waited for us to speak, but there was nothing to say.

She let out a deep breath. "There's more. The longer I'm out of my coma, the more I remember stuff my mother told me. I think I'm supposed to pass it along to you."

"To us?" said Ronny.

"No. I mean Derek," she said. "Last night I thought of a word, and it knocked around my head for a while until I finally said it out loud. But it was my mother's voice that I heard. It was a word she had told me when I was in my coma."

"What word?" I asked, not entirely sure I wanted to know.

"Messenger." Abby paused for a moment. "I think she said that she's some kind of messenger. From there."

"The afterlife?" said Ronny.

Abby nodded. "I mean, she knew about the red

house, even before you got the photo. She knew they're called the Legion. There's probably more, I'm not sure. But I think she's on the good side and she's telling me things you need to know, and so I have to stick close to you."

How was I supposed to deal with that?

"Uh, thanks?" I said, embarrassed.

"Oh, don't thank me!" she said with a quiet laugh. "I don't think I'm going to tell you anything good, but — Ronny, be careful! We want to make it to Coushatta, not crash halfway there!"

Ronny grunted and eased off the accelerator. I was used to his terrifying driving skills by now, but this was Abby's first taste.

"Fine," he said. "But Coushatta is in Red River Parish, two hundred miles from Baton Rouge. I have to stay off main roads because of the police, so you're going to have to sit tight for a few hours."

Sit tight? We had no choice. It was a subcompact.

Hour after hour went by. It was late afternoon, almost five, when we saw a sign for a town called New Compson.

"New Compson was mentioned in the museum display," said Abby. "Amaranthia isn't far away."

"I thought it was just called Compson," I muttered distractedly.

"Why do you say that?" asked Ronny.

I thought about it. "I don't know." That bothered me. It was like an encyclopedia had opened in my brain the instant I heard the name of the house, but there was way too much information, and I couldn't access it fast enough.

"Well, it should be just plain Compson," said Abby, gazing out the window. "There's nothing new about it. Look at those cars! It's like that vintage car museum I saw once with my . . . my . . ."

She didn't finish.

But she was right. The town's main street was scattered with cars and trucks that might have been new thirty, forty, fifty years ago. It looked like the set of an old movie.

"Or maybe Small Compson," said Ronny, with a dark chuckle. "Oops, we missed it."

I think Abby and I both smiled at that. But Ronny was right, too. Even driving slowly, the village blurred past almost before it began. A handful of houses, a gas station, a grocery store, a diner, a stop-light. Then came half a mile of nothing before we saw a dirt area on the shoulder with a small store and an outdoor toilet off the back.

"Stop here," said Abby.

"Not yet," said Ronny. "We're almost —"

"Stop here!" Abby repeated.

Ronny slowed the car and pulled into the dirt lot. The rest stop had a run-down, sinister feel to it.

Like we didn't have enough of that already.

No sooner had Ronny turned off the engine than the little store's screen door filled with the shape of someone huge. I froze and listened closely, but I didn't hear any dead voices. At least not yet.

"I need a snack," Abby announced, hopping out of the car and heading for the store. "And a bathroom."

"You're not going in that store alone," I said.

"So come with."

I followed her across the lot. Abby was good-looking in a plain sort of way, and had the sort of sense of humor that Ronny was losing fast. I didn't mind going with her. But it was sweltering outside, and I was sweating like a hog. I hoped she wouldn't notice.

The big shape had disappeared by the time we reached the screen door. I pulled it open, it squealed, and we entered a tiny store stocked with dust and plenty of nothing else. Standing next to a warped linoleum counter was a large woman in a checkered dress, which hung all the way down to a pair of green rubber fishing boots on her feet. She gripped a sawed-off shotgun lightly, as if it were a toothpick.

"Uh . . . hi," I tried.

"Maybe," the woman said cautiously. "You city folk?"

I tried to grin. "We just came from Baton Rouge."

She hoisted the gun a little higher in her grip. "Pudge."

"Hey! That's not nice," said Abby. "Derek is getting thinner, actually —"

I turned to her. "I am?"

"*Name's* Pudge!" the woman interrupted. "Missy Pudge. People call me Missy."

"Oh," said Abby. Her cheeks flushed pink. Eager to change the subject, she nodded at an open display box on the counter. "Are these candy bars fresh?"

When Missy Pudge laughed, her face shook like pudding. "Would be, if this was 1977!"

Abby bought a peach.

"Wise choice," Missy said, still laughing and pocketing a quarter.

When Abby left to sample the outhouse, I was pretty sure I didn't want to stay in the store alone with the shotgun lady, so I headed outside, too. Ronny was still sitting in the car. I was going to wait with him when I caught sight of the long, dusty hood of a black car parked behind the store.

I stepped closer and saw that the big old car stretched almost the entire length of the store. It was built like a station wagon with a very long back compartment, but it wasn't really a car at all.

It was a hearse.

◄| FIVE |►

What Some Say

"**F**ifty-four Caddy," Missy said, coming up behind me and scratching a patch of gray whiskers on the tip of her chin. "Runs like a top. Hundred twenty miles an hour."

"Nice," I said, silently wondering why a hearse would need to go so fast.

Peering inside the back, I saw a high steel floor laid with runners and little wheels. I guessed that the wheels allowed coffins to slide in and out easily. Draped over the windows were faded velvet curtains tied with tasseled ropes of gold silk. Ornate lamps were mounted on each side, between the floor and ceiling.

"Are those lamps for the dead to read by?" I joked lamely.

"Ha!" Missy exploded with a cheek-wobbling laugh. "Now that's a funny picture! You know, this here limousine used to ferry the Longtempses from their house to the cemetery."

I shivered to hear a stranger mention my mother's family. Before I could say anything, words floated through my brain.

Ferry the dead, the many dead, the recent and the long dead.

"And what you're standing on," she went on, waving her shotgun across the air toward something other than trees and more trees, "this road, this rest stop, this whole land was once part of Amaranthia's Hundred. That's a hundred square miles stretching out from that big old house on both sides of the Red River. The town of Compson used to be on that property, too."

Was that why I had remembered the name?

"Big street in town is called Peace Road," she added, "on account of trying to heal after the riot."

"The riot?"

"Red Monday, 1921," she said. "In my daddy's daddy's day, that town was a hive of wicked folks. Guns, hijacking, killing, you name it. When agents finally came in to bust up the gang, some say they were even worse. Vengeful. Ruthless. Liquor stills exploded, fire swept the town. They call it Red Monday. In all, the riot killed close to two hundred folks, men, women, white, black, and all in between. The Longtempses helped rebuild Compson after. Since then, it's been called New Compson."

Death of two hundred people?

But by fire. Not by water. Maybe they were safe from the Legion.

Then Missy Pudge said, "All drowned."

My heart felt like it was going to fly out of my chest.

"But I thought —"

She laughed. "All comes down to the Red River, don't it? The inferno pushed the fighting all the way to the river. Some say you fight fire with water? Sometimes water don't want to help."

The idea trembled through me. I had to change the subject. "I'd like to see the big house," I said. "I like old houses."

"Ha! Some say the house lies eight, nine miles up the road on the far side of the river." She pointed a gnarled finger off among the oaks. "If you can find it, that is."

"Why wouldn't I be able to find it? It's a big house, isn't it?"

Missy rolled her lips in a strange way, as if she was hungry or surprised. "Folks around here sure don't go looking for it. If they do find it, it doesn't do them any good. Some say that house don't want finding!"

"But that's just some kind of legend, right?" I asked.

"Legend, nothing!" She spat on the ground next to my shoes, then scowled as if upset that she had missed. "I seen it firsthand! My daddy was a mason brought in to put new walks in the garden. From the moment he set foot there, he hated that house, and it hated him right back. Developers, contractors, workmen came and went. The lucky ones were run off by something or other. The unlucky ones just went insane."

Uh-huh. Right. So this was some scary backwoods movie filled with old hearses and nutty folks. Great. Just what I needed. And what was taking Abby so long? I wanted to get out of there.

"Is your father still around?" I asked, edging away slowly, toward Ronny and the car.

"Part of him," Missy said.

A shiver shot up my spine.

"His heart's still as strong as an ox. His mind's the thing that broke. Some say it's because of what he saw at that house one night. All I know is when you talk to him, he says just the one word."

I waited, but Missy Pudge just wiped her large cheeks with the back of her hand and turned away.

"What word?" I asked.

She swung back to face me. "Ghosts! That's the word. My daddy says nothing but 'ghosts' morning, noon, and night. One word is all."

I felt my knees quake.

"Derek —"

Ronny was scowling from the car window. "We have a lot to do." He started the engine. I nodded at Missy and climbed into the tiny car.

Abby finally joined us. "That restroom is no bigger than a coffin. I so want to take a shower."

"You can take five showers tomorrow," snapped Ronny, pulling away from the rest stop. "If we make it."

He slammed his foot on the gas and screeched out onto the road.

⊰ SIX ⊱

The Riverbank

As Ronny raced up the road, his face set hard and eyes piercing the distance, pushing the little car to its limit, Abby leaned up and whispered in my ear.

"Cheery today, isn't he?"

I just nodded. I didn't feel so cheerful myself.

"Great," she muttered. "A couple of silent types." Abby tried to call her Grammy Nora, but reception was spotty. She settled back in her seat with a sigh.

There we were, alone in the middle of nowhere, in a stolen car, with dusk coming soon, looking for a haunted house.

Anyone want to switch places?

I didn't think so.

Over the next eight miles, I told Abby and Ronny about Red Monday and what Missy Pudge had said about the river and Amaranthia. Then Ronny slowed — to Abby's obvious relief — and we started looking for the red house. We couldn't see much. Both sides of the road were thick with oak trees.

"At least we got here before the Legion did," I said. "I usually hear them if they're nearby, but I don't hear anything. I guess we were faster —"

"You think we can win this thing?" Ronny snapped, cutting me off.

"What?"

His face was dark. "You think we can win this thing, don't you? You think the three of us clowns can win against the Legion. No one in the last hundred and fifty years has won against them. We're nothing. There's only one person who ever . . . who . . ." He drifted off.

I glanced at Abby, then back at him. "Ronny? There's only person who ever what?"

He hunched his shoulders, said nothing.

"Ronny?" I said. "Was there someone who fought the Legion and . . . won?"

Ronny glanced back at Abby in the rearview mirror. "What's he talking about?"

"Are you kidding?" she said. "Ronny, you started to tell us something. Did someone stop the Legion?"

"I don't know!" he burst out angrily, shaking his head over and over. "I don't know what you're talking about. Or what I'm talking about. I don't know what I was going to say. It's gone now. Stop asking —"

Before he could finish, I heard a shriek — or a hundred shrieks all at once — and a powerful wind blew out of the woods and sliced across the road. Ronny lost control of the wheel.

"Ronny!" Abby screamed.

The car shot into the ditch, then bounced back onto the road sideways. Ronny slammed on the brakes, which threw up a wall of dust around us.

"What was that —" I started to say.

Then an old green Jeep roared out of the dust, swerving to avoid us. Too late. Its bumper struck our left headlight hard. Glass splashed up into the dusty air. Both car and Jeep spun off into the ditch on the river side of the road.

Ronny twisted the wheel, stomping on the brake, but there was no stopping our car. It bounded down the embankment to the water before striking a tree. The front passenger door cracked open and I flew out, slamming against the ground. The weeds were thick where I fell, but my bad ear was crushed against a rock.

I howled.

Suddenly, almost in slow motion, the Jeep was bouncing down the bank toward me.

"Noooo —" I gasped.

I frantically tried to scramble out of the way, but the Jeep flipped over on its side. The driver screamed as it kept rolling toward me, its right tires spinning wildly.

A wagon's wheel spinning loose at twilight, round and round . . .

I tumbled down the bank to where a narrow stretch of river ran through the hollow at the bottom. Above, the Jeep's front tire caught on a stump, and it flipped now onto its roof, sliding at me backward. I jumped into the water and splashed across as fast as I could.

The Jeep hit the riverbank with a crash and stopped dead. The engine burst loudly.

"Ronny! Abby!" I yelled. No answer. They were far up the bank.

Smoke plumed from under the Jeep's hood. Ignoring it, I crawled to the cab. Inside, an older man with a grizzled face lay twisted across the wheel, his lips in the water, his arms tangled together as if pointing out the back window.

I knew there was nothing to do for him, but I couldn't let him stay like that.

I tried to pull him out, when something suddenly moved in the water outside the cab and splashed across the driver's face. A long, foul gasp blew out from his lips, his eyes bulged open, and his head jerked around.

I screamed.

He had been translated. And he had seen me.

My ear bleeding, I staggered away as quickly as I could. "Ronny! Abby!" I called again, hoping they weren't hurt, hoping they'd hear me. The dead soul groaned louder, angrier, thrashing inside the Jeep. I tried to climb up to the road, but a second storm of air rushed at my face, pushing me back into the water, sweeping me across it to the far side and up into the trees. I could barely see. I finally pushed my way through the thick wall of oaks on the embankment and out onto a vast field.

And there it was.

A giant hulk of a house, standing against the purple sky like a ghostly monument.

All the air in my lungs left at once.

Amaranthia.

⫷ SEVEN ⫸

On the Fields of Defeat

Part of me knew I should turn away from the big red house, charge back through the trees across the water to Abby and Ronny, and tell them all about it.

But I didn't move.

Not in that direction, anyway.

I waded through the weeds toward the house, pulled, like I was in a movie and didn't have control over my character.

"This is not happening," I said to myself.

A step. Another step. Another.

I kept muttering. "That's a big old dark house, Derek. You shouldn't go there alone. Get a grip."

Step. Step. I realized I was soaking wet to my shoulders. I hadn't noticed before. The river must have been deeper than I'd thought.

I moved across the overgrown lawn, into the weaving threads of mist that rose from it. My ear bled, but the pain seemed dull somehow. Through it, I heard:

O scarlet walls, enwall from this nightmare war . . .

Yes! That was it! There was something comforting about the house. I was afraid of it, of course. A haunted house? An abandoned mansion? Anyone would be scared. But there was something hypnotic about the house, too. I wanted to be close to it.

I wanted to be inside it.

I found myself running across what must once have been the great lawn, toward the front steps, when a sound floated across the dusk into my bloody ear. I stopped to listen.

Was it music?

Or just the wind rustling the leaves?

There was no wind.

I heard strings being plucked. I heard bare feet walking on damp planks. I turned to my left and saw a row of cabins built of rough board that I hadn't noticed before. Each one had a peaked roof shingled in oak, and wood smoke rising from side chimneys. From my father's books I knew these were slave quarters, horrible things, but I remembered a story about them. Had Abby read it at the museum? No?

Then where had I heard it?

The story said that the slave houses at Amaranthia were not real slave quarters. The Longtempses used them to cover up what was really going on. At a glance, the family appeared no different from their slave-owning neighbors, but in fact it was smuggling blacks, hundreds of them, out of slavery to the far North of Ohio and Canada.

Had my mother told me this story?

I heard jangling strings and low crooning voices. I thought of Big Bob Lemon, and a lump thickened my throat. He was a huge man, indestructible — I had thought. There was something good and right about having Lemon on your side.

And yet, for all I knew, Bob had died two nights ago.

Another sound now, from my right, but this one clamored in my bad ear — the plinking of iron on iron. I recognized it as the battering of a hammer on an anvil.

Recognized it? When had I ever heard a black-smith pounding an anvil? Never, that's when.

Still, my ear thudded with powerful hammer strokes, pounding out a slow, persistent rhythm. I saw the blacksmith's shop, a dark square of stone, its fireplace flickering orange. Beyond it were the long, low stables.

Out of the corner of my eye, I saw another light. Near the house.

Guttering like a failing candle-flame . . .

I swung around. There was no light. The red house was a dark shape. A dead thing.

My mind was playing tricks on me.

Then a movement in the garden. I saw a man.

Or was that a trick, too? Was it just the evening mist, twisting itself into shapes?

"Am I seriously seeing ghosts now?" I said, trying to laugh at myself. But would it have been so crazy?

I stepped closer.

The man had longish blond hair and wore a crisp gray uniform with a green sash at his waist that glinted in the moonlight. I watched him slide from a dark horse into the arms of a woman in white. Where had she come from? Her face was turned up to his, her long dress plumped out in front. Was she going to have a baby? The hydrangea bushes rustled, and the man turned.

Did I know him?

Was there a photo of him in the museum?

Among the bushes, five, six, or more uniformed riders took shape. Their faces were grim. They had to go.

Their horses' frightened eyes caught the yellow slanting moonlight. The man lowered his face to the woman's. Then, like some glitch in a movie, he was suddenly back on his horse again. He slid down like before, fell into her arms, pressed his face to hers, then was back on the horse.

This crazy, misty scene played over and over. It horrified me. But, beyond the fear, I couldn't help feeling very sad. What exactly was I watching? Was it a dream that wouldn't end? Ghosts caught in a treadmill of moments, unable to escape?

"Seeing ghosts now, Derek?" I said softly. "Just like old Missy Pudge's insane father? Is that what I am?"

No. No way.

I had to find Abby. Find Ronny.

Yet when I turned away from the garden, I found that I was only a few strides from the bottom of the main stairs.

I took in the house in an instant. It was like I had seen it every day of my life — the giant columns, the two galleries, one around the second floor and one around the top, just beneath the roofline.

The main gallery, a deck between the outer columns and the house, was ten feet deep, so the inside rooms wouldn't get direct sunlight. Columns extended from the floor up to the eaves on each side of the house. Two of the columns on a corner of the house had buckled, so the roof and the uppermost gallery sagged below the middle row of windows.

Why I went up the staircase, step by step to the top, I can't say. I don't even remember doing it. But somehow, I was there. The twin front doors, studded with big brass handles and decorated with amaranth carvings, stood right in front of me.

I knew I shouldn't. But I also knew that the old doors, heavy as iron, would swing open for me the instant I pushed. I just didn't know why. I took a deep breath, steadied my feet, and took hold of both handles.

A cry rang out across the lawn from the river.

"Derek! Derek!"

No, I thought. *Please go away.*

"Derek!"

Abby was hurrying toward the house, whipping her cane through the high weeds.

The spell broke like shattering glass. I couldn't hear the sounds from across the fields anymore. Only the dark souls' voices, their chorus of wails and groans, getting closer.

"The Legion —" I started.

"They're here!" Abby cried. "The Legion is attacking New Compson. They're burning it to the ground!"

Ronny wove across the open field in the beat-up car. The front end was bent back into itself, but it still ran. It spun out on the gravel in the garden where I saw no soldier or his wife.

Were they ever really there?

"Get in!" Ronny growled. "We have to help if we can."

Abby pulled me away from the house and pushed me into the back of the car. Ronny slammed his foot on the pedal. We tore across the field.

I looked back and saw that the blacksmith's shop was no more than a pile of stones, the slave houses toppled planks and weeds.

So.

Was it all just an illusion, after all?

Tires spitting up dust like a cyclone, we roared through the tall grass and into the trees.

◄| EIGHT |►

On Peace Road

Ronny angled the car between the hulking oak trees and onto a bridge he'd found buried among them.

Tangled trunks and branches crowded us on both sides, and I lost sight of Amaranthia. It felt as if part of me was still back on the steps of that red house. Would we be able to find the house again? Whatever my key opened was in that house. We had to find it. I had to go back.

But now, I could see a plume of black smoke rising up beyond the road and red flames licking the rooftops of burning houses. I heard the voices of the Legion screeching, moaning in my bad ear.

"There must be fifty of them by now," I said, trying to focus. "I hear them all. They've come for more victims. Missy Pudge said two hundred died on Red Monday, all drowned, escaping the fire."

"The duty of every soldier in the Legion is to grow the army," said Ronny, tearing into the rest stop again. "To do that, they have to supply bodies for the souls waiting to be translated. That's what they did in the bayou. That's what they're doing here." He opened the car door. "I saw some axes behind the rest stop."

Abby and I climbed out of the car and watched him go around the back of the store. He disappeared beyond the hearse, a black lump in the dwindling light.

"You know how to stop them?" I asked when he reappeared.

"I'm going to try," Ronny said, handing me an ax.

It was heavy in my hand, the head a big slab of sharpened steel. I remembered the blacksmith's shop at Amaranthia.

Ronny took an ax himself and held out a third one to Abby. She stepped back. "I have my cane," she said. "I'm not . . . not . . . using one of those things. I'm not a killer."

"They are," said Ronny, heading down the road without looking back, both axes over his shoulder. "All of them are killers. Maybe cutting them up will stop them." He paused. "Cutting . . . there's something I remember . . . something about the neck . . ."

"The *neck*?" Abby said, making a face.

Ronny jammed his eyes closed, then opened them. "There is a way to stop them. A horrible way. I'll remember it later. On foot from here. Be careful. Stay together. Let's go."

When we reached the village, it was a storm of chaos — worse than we'd imagined. New Compson was a grid of streets built around a central square and lined with a few stores, a diner, a gas station, a hotel. The dull shapes of the dead stormed here and there, heaving torches into houses and storefronts, driving the villagers out into the streets. People were screaming, running, staggering in the roaring white glow of the flames.

"Ronny, you know the Legion," said Abby, shielding her eyes from the heat. "How can we —"

"Try to stop any dead soldier you see!" Ronny cried, pointing at a group of five dead men in ragged shorts and T-shirts. I recognized them — tourists translated in Bayou Malpierre. "Hit them, cut them, trip them, slow them down. Do anything —"

A teenage boy ran over to us, carrying a gnarled stick. "Help us stop them!" he said. "I called the police!"

"They're coming from Bienville," shouted a uniformed man with wild hair, hurrying past with his pistol raised. "This is Red Monday all over again!"

As monstrous as the Legion soldiers looked — and you could tell which ones they were right away — they were methodical and calm. That was even more frightening.

"They have rifles in the hardware store!" a woman in a short dress called out. "We have to defend ourselves!" A moment later, a handful of men drove a car straight into the store, breaking the window.

The sound of shattering glass, the rush of water.

I shook my head. Not now.

Alarms sounded. The car reversed, and the crowd clambered over it to ransack the store for guns. I recognized Missy Pudge among them.

"The square!" a man shouted. "Get to the —" His voice was cut off. The heat fell over us like a wall. The sky was orange, white, black.

"Follow me," said Ronny, gripping an ax in each hand. "Don't split up." He turned to me. "I want to see you every minute." We hurried up Peace Road and into the square.

The hotel was on fire. Villagers massed at the Civil War monument on the green. They carried pitchforks, rakes, shotguns, chain saws, rifles. Ronny pushed his way into the center of the crowd.

"Look!" he said, trying to get everyone's attention. He jumped onto the hood of a car whose rear tires were burning. "The people attacking you are already dead. You can't kill them, you can only stop them from killing you! Don't go to the river! The dead come from the water. They want you there. They want you to drown —"

Two ambulances, a police car, and a fire engine screeched into the far side of the square. The dead swarmed them at once.

"He's one of them!" a voice yelled out, and someone threw something at Ronny, smacking his forehead. He slid to his knees on the car hood. Abby rushed to him.

"No!" I jumped up onto the car hood. "We're trying to —"

"Derek!" Abby cried, helping Ronny to his feet. "Tell them who you are!"

"What?" I didn't know what she meant. Then it hit me.

"I'm a Longtemps — Derek Longtemps Stone! That's my house over there. Amaranthia!"

Amid the inferno, the crowd hushed. In that hush, I heard the voice of Erskine Cane echoing in my bad ear. Three words.

He is here.

Cane meant me. I knew it.

The crowd stared at me, a hundred souls, black and white, men, women, and children. I had never been so frightened in my life.

"I —"

But I didn't get any further.

A pump at the gas station on the square exploded. I fell from the car. The crowd ran for cover.

The dead — fifty or more — charged after us, howling. Their voices crashed into my ear.

"This way," said Ronny.

The three of us scrambled behind the diner, which had escaped the fire so far. Old tires, the crumpled fender of a truck, and three cracked radiators were strewn on the ground. Overturned garbage. Rats.

I dropped to my knees, exhausted. Cane's steely voice stung my bad ear again. *Take them from their houses. He is here.* Then the sound of engines, low and rough, as trucks were driven straight into houses — glass exploded, wood snapped, the roaring engines popped from the heat.

And voices, screaming: "To the river! Save your-selves from the fire! To the river!"

"No, no," said Ronny, over and over and over.

The sound of shattering glass, the rush of water.

We raced out from behind the diner again, desper-ate to help, and it all stopped.

People ran, houses burned, Ronny and Abby yelled, but for me it stopped when I saw them.

Erskine Cane. Twitchy. Waldo Fouks.

I stood amid the chaos of Peace Road, and I couldn't move. Cane had just spoken, but Twitchy went running off with a torch as if he didn't hear. All at once, Cane spun forward and wrapped his mas-sive arms around Twitchy's head. Cane twisted his arms swiftly. I gagged as Twitchy squirmed and uttered a long groan. I saw something come rushing out of the back of his head like a patch of dark air. There was a shriek, then Twitchy went still. The big soldier opened his hands, and the body fell, dark and unmoving, to the middle of the road.

Waldo's blind eyes squinted skyward. He was shaking. "You cut him. . . ."

And now I'd seen how the animated dead die. Ronny was right. It was horrible.

"The First has called me," said Cane. "I rule here."

Whatever jumble of ideas, questions, and nightmares I'd had about the Legion was clarified in that instant, when I saw Cane and Waldo on the street.

Maybe there was the First, but right now the dead had only one leader.

Ruthless, stark, deadly, Cane towered over the blind boy and spoke. "The First has commanded. Grow the Legion, stop the young captain. I hear the enemies. They are close. Three of them. The boy has the key."

The young captain?

He turned to a handful of dead men, some of whom were Waldo's smugglers. One by one, they nodded.

"Take the humans to the river," Cane said to Waldo.

"Use the trucks. I will burn the red house. The First has commanded it."

Cane spoke in a slow monotone, as if each word was carefully thought out.

I was frozen where I stood. No one saw me.

I watched Cane stomp away, knowing I'd just seen the brutal leadership of the Legion.

I hadn't seen the First, but Cane blindly obeyed him, and that frightened me more than anything else I'd seen so far.

And *three* enemies? He was talking about us. Ronny, sure. He was translated. And I already knew if my bad ear allowed me to hear the dead, somehow the dead could hear me. But Abby? How could he hear Abby? Or was it someone else? Who was the third?

"Ronny!" I whispered over my shoulder. "Abby!"

No answer.

Waldo shrieked orders to a handful of the dead, fear dripping from his blind eyes. The Legion soldiers dragged victims into the trucks. They were headed for the river where — I knew — the untranslated dead, the killers and hijackers, had been waiting since Red Monday. To return.

I staggered away, found Ronny and Abby in the empty streets.

"He knows we're here," I told them. "We need to get to the house. Cane's going to burn it. I have to find what the key opens now!"

Ronny growled.

"Derek's right," Abby said softly. "We need to go to Amaranthia."

"Then there's nothing more for us here," Ronny said finally.

We looked only long enough to see the dead moving toward the river, their faces blackened, their clothes smoking, their eyes focused on some horrible future.

The soldiers were doing their duty. The Legion was growing. How many would there be by nightfall? A hundred? Two hundred?

More?

◀ NINE ▶

To the Red House

We tore up the road toward Amaranthia, the car rattling like it might fall to pieces at any minute. Ronny didn't seem to care if he made it worse by driving like a crazy person, until two tires blew. The car finally died for good in a roadside ditch.

"Oh, man, oh, man, oh, man," Abby said under her breath.

Ronny climbed out and kicked the flat tires. "We'll have to hoof it from here."

"Take the hearse," I said, pointing back toward the rest stop. "It's our only chance to get there before the Legion."

Ronny looked back. "Fine. Hurry."

We hustled along the road, hearing the wail of sirens racing up from the south.

When we reached the rest stop, I searched the store and found Missy Pudge's keys below the register. I was a regular car thief now. Fantastic. Ronny had taught me well.

We wrenched open the hearse doors. They squealed like the voices of the dead. Appropriate. We climbed in, and Ronny started the engine. It rumbled to life. He jerked the stick into reverse, and we pulled onto the road with a shriek of rubber.

We raced up the road in silence, passing the junked car, then passing the green Jeep in the embankment. I sensed it was empty. The dead driver had freed himself.

We drove along the bank for a while, then veered narrowly between two trees and over the bridge Ronny had found before.

I felt dizzy and drained as we rolled over the old stones toward the house.

Stone road, cold road, road to time long past . . .

I hated the words in my head. "Faster," I said. "Missy said this car can could do a hundred twenty miles an hour."

"Not through the woods it can't," Ronny said. Less than a minute later, he jerked the hearse to a stop in the weeds, a hundred feet from the red house.

"Inside, before they get here," he instructed.

"Flashlights?" Abby asked. "It'll be dark in there."

Ronny shrugged. "Try the glove box."

She banged the glove compartment open with the heel of her hand. "Two," she said. "In case they need to bury someone at night, I guess. Only one of them works."

"Bring it," said Ronny. "There are probably candles inside, if the rats haven't eaten the wax. We need to find what that key opens, then scram. Cane and the others will be here soon. I want to be long gone when they show up."

My head was a fog. When the two of them climbed out of the hearse, I sat staring at the red house like a kid at his first drive-in movie. I couldn't move.

"Get out," said Ronny sharply.

Of course. I knew I had to.

But I also knew that the moment I set foot inside Amaranthia, I would be lost to it. I would be in that trance again. Seeing things. Hearing voices. I was scared to death. Of the house. Of Cane. Of everything. Why couldn't I move?

O scarlet walls, enwall from this nightmare war . . .

"Get out," Ronny repeated. "The Legion will be here so fast, your head will spin."

"Okay," I said. I thought of Twitchy's head. I still couldn't move.

"Or just stay there and give me the key —"

"Back off, soldier," said Abby, flashing Ronny a look. She reached into the car and pulled my arm gently. "Derek, we don't have time for this. Come on."

Drawing a long breath, I slid off the seat, moved toward the stairs and those giant front doors. The hammering of horseshoes, the strumming of guitars, the warbling voices across the fields — they were nothing now. Darkness and silence. Scattered stones, loose bricks, weeds. The soldier and his young wife were only mist in the moonlight.

Ronny was pacing the high grass like a madman. He finally clamped his hand on my arm and pulled both Abby and me onto the stairs. We all went up together.

At the top they stepped aside, and for the second time I took the door handles in my shaking fingers.

But this time I turned them and pushed. The doors swung in, and the house gasped out a stale breath of welcome.

⊰ TEN ⊱

Dead Air

The air, thick and heavy, was worse than no air at all. My throat stung. I barely breathed.

I don't know why, but I had an overwhelming urge to shut the doors and seal us off from the outside world. No sooner had we stepped through them than I took hold of the inside knobs and pushed the doors closed.

"Okay, this isn't going to turn into some creepy teen movie, is it?" Abby said, flicking on her flashlight.

"No." I paused. "It's been a creepy teen movie for a month already."

She narrowed her eyes at me, then shone her light into the dark house.

The first thing we saw was a staircase, sweeping up from the entryway in a wide curve. The walls on either side were hung with faded portraits. Confederate soldiers. Young women. Old women with faces dry as paper, dressed in black. They were widows, I knew. I had seen them in my father's Civil War books, dressed in what were called "widows' weeds" — black dresses, black bonnets, white lace at the neck and wrists. Had all their husbands died in the war?

"Look for something small," said Abby, bringing me crashing back to reality.

"It's not going to be easy," Ronny said darkly. "The rooms are mostly empty. Looted by squatters, probably."

"A chest. A box. A drawer," she went on. "Maybe even a wall panel. This house is probably full of secret passages. Look for anything with a lock on it."

"We should split up," said Ronny. "This house has thirty rooms, at least. Besides, the voices are getting closer. I hear Waldo's crazy shrieking. They'll be here soon."

Ronny could hear the voices of the Legion. In some part of my head, I could hear them, too, just as I had since the train accident. But there were other sounds now. Other voices. And not just those crazy lines of poetry that kept popping in for a visit. Voices I hadn't heard before. Old voices, chanting from the darkness.

You . . . see . . . you . . . see . . .

I looked at Ronny and Abby to check if they heard them, too. They didn't react. Great. Like Waldo Fouks said, I'm special.

I shook my head to clear the voices, but they only got sharper, more insistent.

You . . . see . . . !

See what? Maybe my hurt ear was playing more tricks on me. Why not? Load it on. Make me crazier than I already am.

Plink . . . plink . . .

Through a cracked door to the right, I saw the shambles of what I somehow knew was the everyday parlor. The wreck of an ancient upright piano leaned against the wall. Its keys sounded randomly, as if fingered by ghostly hands. The sound made me shiver.

Plink . . . plink . . .

Then I spotted a large gray mouse, hobbling on three legs back and forth across the keys.

"What? No ghost?" Abby said shakily, trying to be funny.

No one laughed.

I thought of the soldier and his bride in the garden. Were they really ghosts? Had I really seen them at all?

"Yuck," Abby went on, filling the silence. "This place makes me want to shower for a week. Here's a candle. You take it." Using matches on the table next to it, she lit it. I took the candlestick.

"Get moving, you two," Ronny snarled. "I'm going upstairs. Whoever finds something, yell. And Derek, have the key ready. Don't lose it in the dark, all right?"

"He won't lose it," Abby scoffed. Then she turned to me and whispered, "Do not lose that key!"

We split up at the bottom of the big staircase. Abby headed left, Ronny went up the steps, and I walked straight ahead, underneath the curving stairs.

I had no idea what I would find that way, but going under the stairs seemed right somehow. I took a step, another, under the stairs and around a corner into the north wing of the house. The whole way, the air was like wool, suffocating and heavy.

Then the scratching started.

It came from behind the wall to my right, and it sounded like fingernails scraping on wood. I jerked away, cringing, and the scratching was behind me. Then it was beneath the floor at my feet, as if something were looking up through the boards.

The voices were back. Whispers, hissings, all in my bad ear.

You . . . see . . . you . . . see . . .

"I don't see! Get away from me!" I must have hit my ear harder than I thought in the car crash.

I hurried back — I thought — to where Abby was. The darkness and shadows confused me, and I didn't find her. But the scratches found me, scuttling behind the old wood like an army of rats. My skin crawled. Was someone there? Was the house alive?

I found a small room, a little office no bigger than a pantry. It smelled like oil and dead flowers. A broken chair and a small table draped with a rug sat under a window.

I checked the table for drawers. It had none, but a pair of eyes flashed out from under the draped rug. I'm not proud of it, but I think I screamed. A shape the size of a cat skittered out from beneath the table.

A raccoon.

Surprised by me, too, the raccoon jumped back under the table. I kicked the table legs, expecting the creature to run past me to the hallway. But it didn't. There was only a muffled scuffling in the wall behind the table as the animal hurried away.

I pulled the table away from the wall, its legs shrieking against the floorboards. The raccoon was nowhere in sight. In the candlelight, I saw that the wall panel behind the table was hinged. The raccoon had disappeared behind it.

I pried it open.

A passage ran the length of the house behind the wall. I held up the candle and saw struts, planks, studs, and bricks disappearing into the distance. An occasional round piece of glass, like the bottom of a flat bottle, was set in the walls, and clouded moonlight fell into the length of the passage.

I knew it was a bad idea, but I couldn't stop myself. I stumbled forward on boards at first, then stone, as the passage dipped below the level of the first floor of the house. Sour air wafted up from somewhere below.

Glass shattered on the floor above me. "Derek?" It was Abby, muffled and far away.

"Abby?" I said. She couldn't have heard, I was so quiet. Like in the bayou, I couldn't raise my voice.

I was quiet, but the passage was breathing with voices.

Forward!

Come!

Go!

One rumbly old voice reminded me of Bob Lemon's. *Never, no, never . . .*

Then several women's voices rose over the others, chanting those words again. *You . . . see . . . you . . . see . . .* It was a chorus, moving in and out like waves at the shore. Other voices broke through, all of them burbling in the darkness.

Who are you, boy?
Don't steal our silver, please, it's all we have —
We have waited so long, so very long . . .
And again: *Who are you, boy?*

"Enough!" I cried, pushing past them. By the time I reached the end of the passage, I was a good two feet lower than where I started. I froze. In my candle's glow I could see a set of stairs leading down into darkness.

Then I saw a hand. A hand? No. There was nothing there. I was imagining it. I leaned onto the top step, steadied myself on the banister.

I felt something brush the hair on the back of my hand.

"No. No way," I whispered. Closing my eyes, I imagined another hand placing itself lightly upon the banister. It was a woman's, old, shriveled, white, a fringe of lace at the wrist. A widow's hand. It slid down the banister slowly.

"This is crazy!" I said aloud, opening my eyes and seeing nothing. But it was happening. I knew it. I was being sucked into this weird old house, hearing things, seeing things. Impossible things. Ghosts.

Two old shapes formed, three, four, their shrunken white faces marked with the black smudge of death, their cheeks carved with silver tears.

The Widows' Pledge! said one. Then a second voice

joined in, then all of them, a chorus of old voices. *The Widows' Pledge!*

I knew they weren't really there, but in my mind they were all around me. We descended the stairs together, a parade of widows and me. They were chanting, over and over.

You . . . see . . . you . . . see . . .

"No, I still don't see," I whispered. My throat felt like sandpaper.

Step by step by step, I went down the stairs, until my foot struck the floor with a thud. Moonlight, silver and pale, fell on a network of arches and columns surrounding a big white stone house.

So that was it.

I had found the crypt.

⊰ ELEVEN ⊱

What the Key Opens

I was in the basement of the house. The floor was laid with brick, but it was uneven, as if the bricks were set directly on the ground. Big wooden beams supported the floor above.

Moonlight filtered down from small barred windows high in the walls, and I saw tattered cobwebs hanging over the white stone tomb.

It was a crypt, like the others I'd seen in recent days — in St. Louis Cemetery in New Orleans, in the ancient boneyard in Bayou Malpierre. It smelled like water and death and age.

. . . that bitter perfume of death.

Good thing I hadn't eaten all day.

Somewhere in the dark — or in my mind — I heard the widows murmur again.

"Quiet, already," I said, but I'd said it so softly I wondered if I'd actually said it aloud.

I gripped the candlestick. I wanted to feel it pinch

the softness of my fingers and wake me from this gauzy dream.

"I'm Derek Stone!" I insisted to myself. "I hate this stuff. Up is up! Down is down! I don't believe in ghosts."

But nothing changed.

The widows murmured on. *You . . . see . . .*

The tomb walls were carved with the same flower design I'd seen on everything else in the house. Amaranths. Only here, black mold had crawled inch-thick over the stone, pitting the alabaster.

Fixed on the crypt door was a small gilt oval frame and, inside it, an old photograph of a young man, a soldier.

With light locks dangling to his shoulders, a thin mustache, and a beard on his chin, he looked solemnly at the camera. On his shoulders were epaulets and tassels.

It was the same soldier I had seen in the garden. But how did I know what he looked like before even seeing the photograph? And who was he, anyway?

The widows hushed their mumbling for a second, then started again.

In the photo the young man was stern-faced. But for some reason, I imagined him smiling, moving, alive, and — oddly — I imagined his hair parted on the other side.

"Whatever," I said to the dark. I really was losing it.

The stone door of the crypt had a handle mottled with green rust. I turned it, pulled it toward me. The big white door slid open easily.

Not a good sign.

The widows' murmuring grew louder.

Inside the tomb, on a high stone pedestal, lay a black oak coffin. Its lid was just above eye level.

Holding my shrinking candle high, I made myself enter the crypt. Starting on the right, I walked completely around the dusty coffin until my legs refused to move anymore. From there, I could see a brass plate with the same amaranth design as the key in my pocket. The plate had a slot in it, a lock, set into the coffin just under the edge of the lid.

I breathed out.

So this was it. The coffin of some hundred-and-fifty-year-old dead guy I didn't even know?

"But the key might not work," I said aloud, trying to make sense of it all. "It might not even work on this lock."

Only I couldn't stop my fingers from running over

the delicate scrollwork surrounding the lock. I knew I had to try it.

While the widows murmured on — *You . . . see . . .* — I pulled the old key from my pocket and slowly slid it into the lock.

It went in all the way to the handle.

My chest froze, my stomach throbbed.

Somewhere, in the corner of my mind, I heard footsteps tramping across the floor over my head. *Thump. Thump.* I thought of Abby. Was she searching for me — or running for her life? Never mind. I had to do this. I couldn't leave yet.

Resting the candlestick on the coffin lid, I gripped the key firmly and turned.

The lock clicked.

⊰| TWELVE |⊱

The Red Stain

I stood motionless by the coffin for a long time. The only sound I heard was the echo of that *click*.

Placing the candlestick on the corner of the pedestal, I took the lid of the casket in both hands and lifted as far as I could until, with a muffled squeak, it stayed open. The air inside was stale, old, dry. I tried not to breathe it in.

Shreds of satin lining hung like silver moss from the inside of the lid. At first, nothing was visible over the top. My heart skipped. Was the coffin empty? Maybe the key meant nothing at all.

But I had to look inside.

Standing on my toes, I peered over the edge of the casket, and my stomach flipped. Inside was a uniform of rags. A fleshless skull was tipped back on the sunken remains of a sickly brown pillow. Crumbled vertebrae snaked into the woolen collar of a military jacket. My throat thickened. It was disgusting. But I couldn't take my eyes away. Was this all that remained of the bright young man in the photograph? The gallant soldier in the garden?

"Who are you?" I said softly.

The widows' voices paused again, but only for an instant.

The bones of his fingers were folded over his sunken chest in the same way as knights I'd seen in cathedral crypts. But clutched between them was something wrapped in a faded green cloth. I knew it was the sash — emerald green silk trimmed with a half-disintegrated shred of gold tassel — of a Civil War cavalry officer. I'd seen photos of those sashes in my dad's old books, and the soldier had worn it in the garden.

The sash was folded tightly around something the size of a small, flat box. I couldn't tell you why, but my fingers itched to hold the thing, whatever it was. And, weirdly, I felt as if the chanting widow ladies echoing in my crazy, jumbled head expected me to take it.

Had they led me down here for just that reason?

So now I was doing what ghosts wanted me to? Yeah, I was far gone, all right.

I gently slid the object out from under the fleshless fingers. I pressed it against my own chest and stepped away from the coffin, lowered the lid, locked it, pocketed the key. Taking my candle, I walked backward out of the crypt, feeling like the thing I had found, whatever it was, was what I'd been searching for my whole life.

Standing in a pale blade of moonlight, I carefully unwrapped the sash. Inside was a leather pouch — scratched, worn, and as brittle as old wood. A flap over the top was snapped in place. When I unwound its narrow leather straps, I recognized the pouch as a Civil War cartridge box.

The letters CSA were stamped into the flap.

"Confederate States of America," I said to myself.

So what was inside? Old rifle shells? Pistol bullets? Ammunition to use against the Legion?

No.

I snapped open the cartridge box carefully. Inside was a small, leather-bound book with an amaranth design pressed into the leather. I lifted the cover of the book. Snaked across the first page, from bottom left to top right, was a dark stain tinged with red. Dried blood.

Written in a dense black scrawl across the page, I read:

The Ghost Road
A Poem of the Long War
by
Capt. Ulysses Perceval Longtemps

Captain? Erskine Cane had said he was searching for the young captain.

I didn't breathe, I couldn't, as I ran my fingers across the inked words.

Ulysses Perceval Longtemps . . .

The name shivered through me. He was a relative, okay, but had I ever heard the name before? As far as I could remember, I hadn't. But in my mind, the name sounded like the shattering of glass and the long drawn notes of a violin.

"Ulysses Perceval Longtemps . . ." I said aloud, barely a whisper.

All at once I sensed the widows emerging from the shadows, floating closer to me. Then again, in that room of death, the quivering moonlight made it seem like everything was moving. They murmured their words over and over, and I finally understood. They weren't saying *you . . . see . . . you . . . see . . .* at all. They were saying *Ulysses*.

But why? My throat went dry.

I turned the page over to the beginning of the long poem, and read its first words:

Within your crimson walls, I was an angel child . . .

Blood drained from my head. I wobbled.

I knew those words! I'd heard them over and over in my mind since the train wreck. Seeing them here in my hands, I felt like I was being pulled overboard. And I remembered the next lines as I read them:

From room to room I floated in your wingless window light,

And yet gray Evil, like a wolf, from shadows sprang . . .

I snapped the book closed.

"No!" I shouted to the darkness. "I can't know these stupid words —"

There was a scuffling sound on the dusty floor above. The voices vanished like fog in a wind. My candle blew out, and the pale moonlight clouded over outside, plunging the crypt black.

"Derek?" came a whisper.

I jumped. Was this voice real? Or ghostly, like the others?

"Derek?"

It came from the top of the wooden stairs. "Derek, are you down there in the dark?"

"Abby?" I said softly, still dazed.

"Derek!" she cried, sounding relieved. "Is Ronny with you?"

"Ronny?" It took me a moment. "No. He's not —"

"Then get up here fast," she said. "He's gone. I think the Legion is already in the house, and they've got him —"

"They've got . . ." I said, unbelieving. Footsteps thudded on the floorboards. Ronny's bloodcurdling scream cut through the dead air of the room.

"Ronny!" I shouted.

I swallowed a thousand questions, stuffed the book and sash into the cartridge box, slung it over my shoulder, and hurried up the stairs to Abby. The spell of the crypt was shattered.

"I'm coming!"

⊰ THIRTEEN ⊱

On the Gallery

Crashing, yelling, feet pounding through the passage. Abby grabbed my arm and wouldn't let go, pulling me up the stone steps after her.

"You found something?" she said breathlessly, eyeing the pouch slung over my shoulder.

"A book," I said, already winded. You'd think I would have gotten better at this whole running-from-the-dead thing by now.

"What book?"

"How did you find me?" I asked, pushing off the question. "How —"

"I . . ." she started. "I don't know. I just knew you were down there. This house. My mother."

"Your mother?" I said, still struggling to keep up. The girl with the cane was faster than me.

"There's some connection between us. Don't ask me how, but for some reason, I usually know where you are. This is so completely not the way my life is supposed to go —"

She glanced back at me. "What's the book?"

I didn't know how to explain it, the words in my head, the words in the book.

"Derek, hello? You still in there?"

I shook my head. "Later. Later!"

We rushed out of the passage, through the little study, and out under the stairs. Abby stifled a scream.

A man whose clothes hung in charred tatters stood in the main hall. A New Compson townsman — translated. His head swiveled toward us, toward me, toward the pouch. A grin. Black teeth.

"Found!" he cried.

Pushing Abby ahead of me up the stairs, I stumbled and fell back into the guy. The smell from his open mouth was nauseating. I kicked wildly, catching him in the shoulder, and Abby swung her cane at his head. He fell back, eyes bulging in anger.

"This way!" Abby called, yanking me up the stairs with her.

Ronny's cries were moving quickly, somewhere far above us. We rushed up another flight of stairs to the top floor.

"Ronny!" We threw ourselves at the nearest door. It popped open in time for us to see a troop of dead men drag Ronny through a window onto the balcony outside. Waldo was barking orders at them.

"Get out there!" I yelled, lunging for the window.

"No! No," said Abby. "This way!" She pulled me back to the hallway.

"What — Abby —"

"This way!" she insisted. "Cut them off."

I followed her down the hallway. She pushed through door after door until we reached the side of the house. The gallery outside was empty.

"He's not here," I said.

Her face was odd, twisted. "This is where we should . . . let's get outside —"

"How do you —"

"She's here. My mother. With Ronny. I know it." Abby tried the windows. They were hopelessly stuck. I cast around and saw a poker in the fireplace. With both hands, I swung it hard at the nearest window, then ran it around the edges to break whatever wooden slats and glass remained.

We scrambled through the window onto the gallery outside. It squealed with our weight, sagging between us and the corner.

"This won't hold us," I said. "It's going to break —"

But there he was.

Ronny was held up limply by a handful of Legion soldiers, Waldo at their head. My brother's face was a mask of terror, his legs twisted under him. His eyes fell on the cartridge box, and he knew. "Derek, don't say anything! Nothing! Get that out of here!"

"I knew you would find it," Waldo squeaked. How did he know? His blank eyes searched my face. "You really are a special Longtemps, aren't you? Now give it to me, or we cut the boy from his soul."

Cut. I could tell by Ronny's face that he must have remembered what it meant to be cut.

"We're not leaving you, Ronny," I said, still holding the poker. "And you're not getting this, Waldo."

Waldo's blind eyes drilled into mine. Behind him were some of the dead villagers from New Compson. Their faces were wet, gray, smoking. I knew they had drowned at the river.

Waldo nodded his little head, and a Legion soldier knocked Ronny in the chest. My brother fell limp to the gallery floor.

"You —" I stepped forward, Abby next to me. The planks under our feet cracked loudly.

"Give us what you found," Waldo commanded. I felt for the cartridge box hanging at my waist.

What you found? So he didn't know what it was?

"No," I said as calmly as I could. I took Abby by the arm. A dark shape moved behind Waldo. I smelled decay and knew who it was.

Erskine Cane's wife.

In the body of Abby's mother.

Even before she got a clear view of her mother, Abby began wobbling. "Oh, no . . ."

"I'm sorry. I should have told you," I whispered.

"Cut the boy," Waldo ordered.

"No!" I said. My heart turned to ice as Abby's mother slid out from behind Waldo. She was worse than before. Her legs were no larger or stronger than planks of old wood beneath her ragged dress. Her arms were rods of white bone, her face draped with flesh the color of dirty milk.

But she hoisted Ronny's limp body in one powerful arm. Her gray hands clamped his head. Ready to twist? To cut him?

"No!" I burst out. "Here it is, take it —"

I moved to throw the book to Waldo, but Abby's mother pushed forward, screeching in my ears like a teapot ready to explode. "First! Find the — First! One day only — one day!"

Abby gasped. "She's talking to *you*, Derek."

All at once, with inhuman strength, her mother hurled Ronny across the sagging gallery at us. Waldo wailed and lunged at the woman with his creepy little hands, like he was going to cut her himself. She wriggled free and threw herself onto the lowest part of the gallery, splintering the planks between us. It started to rip away from the house.

Without thinking, I smashed the window next to me with the poker. Not knowing where I got the strength, I pushed Ronny through to the room inside.

"Abby, get back!" I shouted as the boards cracked beneath our feet.

"Mom!" Abby cried, reaching out for her mother. Their hands touched. The wood splintered. The railing snapped.

"Get in here!" I screamed. I threw one arm tightly around Abby's waist and pushed her through the window, falling in after her.

Waldo and the others skittered back to the corner as the gallery plummeted away from the house, taking Abby's mother to the ground with it.

Abby was screaming and trembling like a leaf on the floor of the room. All at once, she jumped to the window. We saw her mother's motionless shape on the ground. Her face gray with horror, Abby cried out over and over, "Mom! Mommy!"

Then her mother moved. She twisted on the ground like a wounded animal, then jerked awkwardly to her feet, and, with a single look back at Abby, stomped away toward the woods. She picked up speed, finally running away from the house until she was gone.

"She's —" Abby started, then broke down in tears.

"Come on," I managed to say, pulling her toward the door and dragging Ronny to his feet. "We have to go."

⊰ FOURTEEN ⊱

Wings of a Carved Angel

Coming to and spotting the cartridge box slung over my shoulder, Ronny was suddenly as alert as a soldier in battle.

"Downstairs!" he barked. "We have what we need. Let's go!"

We barreled after him. Abby was still sobbing, but she kept up as best she could. "She escaped. She's out there. Derek, my mother's out there!"

"I know," I said.

I didn't know where her mother would go or what she would do, only that she had saved Ronny.

And the book.

Ronny led us down to the second-floor landing. We'd planned to get all the way out of the house, but we pulled up short.

Erskine Cane stormed out from a side hall with the gray-haired man, the one-armed conductor, and a dozen others, blocking our way. He held an unlit torch. On him, a torch was more terrifying than a cannon.

"I want the book!" he demanded, stomping toward us like a machine.

He knows it's a book, I thought. *What else does he know?*

Ronny grabbed the poker that I'd been too distracted to put down, and threw it at Cane's head — not doing any damage, just distracting him.

"Run!" Ronny said, reaching for Abby's hand. "The back hall!"

He and Abby took off with me close behind. I followed the sound of their footsteps in the dark, stumbled, the dead stomping after me. Soon I heard only my own footsteps. I slowed.

"Ronny? Abby?" I whispered.

No answer.

What part of the house was I in now?

I tried to breathe slowly, clutched for the cartridge box. Still there. But Ronny and Abby were nowhere. Or maybe I was nowhere.

A draft of cool air brushed my cheek, and I turned to face it.

This way . . .

Them again. The voices. I didn't want to listen, but the hallway behind me suddenly thudded with footsteps, so I slipped into a tall room. It was empty except for a cast-iron staircase, narrow, with a busted railing only halfway up. It led to a ceiling a good twenty feet high.

I pushed the door closed behind me. The stomping feet of the dead passed. Why hadn't they heard me?

You are both with us . . .

Both?

The staircase creaked, quivered in the still air. Was I supposed to go up the stairs?

Beyond the top step, I saw a door. Was someone behind it?

Come . . . come . . . you . . . see . . .

Was it his room?

Was it Ulysses Longtemps's room?

I set my foot on the first iron step. The whole staircase swayed under my weight. It was like stepping onto a boat. It made me dizzy, but I climbed up the spiral stairs, round and round, higher and higher. The closer I got to the top, the more clearly I saw that the stairs had broken away from the landing. Every step I took pulled them farther from the wall.

When I reached the top, I hoisted myself off the uppermost step and onto the small landing.

I pushed the door. It opened onto a small, windowed room at the very top of the roof, like the *faux chambre* in my old house in New Orleans. The house that Erskine Cane burned down. It seemed like so long ago since I had been there, even though it had only been a few days.

Was this my life now? Running? Hiding? Would it ever stop moving long enough for me to understand it?

Red damask curtains, looking as heavy as iron sheets, draped the walls between the windows. Almost every window was broken, letting in the gauzy yellow moonlight and hot night air.

On either side of an empty mantelpiece was a place for an ornament. On the right one stood a carved angel, painted gold. I knew that angel. The left space was empty.

So.

The golden angel where the key had been hidden had come from this room. The angel on top of my house in New Orleans had once been here. But why? I dug in my pocket for the key, clutched it tight.

I could never have been in this little room before. Of course not. But I knew it was Ulysses Perceval Longtemps's room. Without thinking, I bent down to a panel on the left of the door. My fingers found a small gash that I knew had been made when Ulysses was sixteen and practicing saber. He had cut his arm that day.

I suddenly wanted to get out of there. This was all too much. I wanted my mind back.

Hushhhhh.

The flowery scent of magnolia wafted through the room. It brought me back to the museum. I'd smelled it there, and long before that, too.

In my mind, I saw the narrow streets of the City of the Dead, St. Louis Cemetery in New Orleans, ten years earlier. The ghost scent of magnolia had floated there, too. I remembered my little hand held firm in another's warm grip.

The floorboards creaked, and the fragrance fell over me. Had it drifted into the room through the windows?

No. It wasn't from outside.

A whisper of movement, the sound of fabric drawn aside, and I wasn't alone.

◄| FIFTEEN |►

Just Like Old Times

A shape moved from shadow to shadow, and soon a face framed by long black hair formed in the moonlight.

The scent of magnolia bloomed in the small room.

"Who are you?" I asked.

No answer. But I knew.

The shape took a step, cutting into the pale light.

My throat tightened. "Who —"

"Derek, honey . . ."

I froze inside. Said nothing.

"Derek, honey, it's me."

I said nothing. Nothing. And then . . .

"Mom?"

"I'm here, honey."

It all came out in a rush of words. "Mom? Mom! What are you doing here? I haven't seen you for ten years. And . . . your perfume! I smelled it at the museum this morning, before the explosion. It was you. You were there! But you're supposed to be in France. Dad said you were in France —"

"Derek, your father —"

"And before that," I interrupted. "I smelled it in the cemetery when I was young. I remember."

"Derek, your father . . ." she repeated softly, then stopped.

"Dad? What about Dad?" My father's face swam in my mind. I imagined his damaged hand, his deep, tired eyes. I didn't know how he had survived the train wreck — I didn't know if he really had. And here was my mother, after ten years, talking about him. "What about Dad?"

"Don't . . ."

She stopped again.

"Don't what? Mom. Tell me."

"Don't trust him, Derek. He was at the war memorial. He's been following you. I —"

"Following me?" I practically screamed, shaking all over. "What are you talking about? Are you serious? Don't trust *him*? I don't trust you!" I heard yelling from the floors below, echoing footsteps. "You left me, Mom. You ran away. I was only four. Don't trust *him*? You can't be serious —"

"Deadly serious, Derek. I had to keep him away from you. The explosion —"

"That was you?" I said. "But how?"

"I had to keep him away from you, Derek. And I've come here to tell you why."

"This is crazy," I spat. My hands grabbed at the air in front of me, as if trying to shake something loose. Then I felt the key, cutting into my palm.

"This old key," I said slowly. "You hid it in the angel on the roof in New Orleans, didn't you? You put it there."

"The key was hidden in that angel long ago, Derek, by someone other than me." Her eyes glanced at the empty spot next to the mantel. "I had it put on the roof when your father decided to turn the *faux chambre* into his room. It would be safe up there until it was needed."

She spoke as if we had talked every morning and night for the last ten years. I hadn't laid eyes on her that whole time, hadn't heard her voice on the telephone, hadn't seen so much as a photograph of her.

"Needed? What for? To find this book?"

She put her hands out, palms up. "This is where he was laid out, you know. His things were right here, where we're standing."

My mind was a storm of questions.

"Ulysses loved it up here," she went on before I could get anything out. "The Finial, he called it. 'I'm going up to the Finial now,' he'd say. 'I'll be in the Finial until dinnertime.' He was like that."

I was shaking all over. "You talk like you knew him."

Her black hair stirred in some movement of air I didn't feel. "Ulysses Perceval Longtemps was the soul of this house, even after he left it. From the moment he could walk and talk, anyone who lived here — as I did, when I was young — knew him like a brother."

A brother? A dead rebel soldier brother. I guess that would have seemed weirder to me before the train crash. A lot of things would.

"Or a son," she added in a whisper.

My mother moved through the shafts of moonlight, then stopped to run her fingers along the gash in the panel I had noticed earlier. "Ulysses was blessed with gifts unimaginable for a young man of his time. He was an engineer, a surgeon, a poet. And then came that horrible war. Ulysses was only twenty-four when he died. The war changed him forever."

I thought of Ronny and knew it was true. War did that.

Some part of me recognized noises in the house below. Shouting. A cry. Wood splintering.

"His soldiers gave his widow the poem he was writing when he died. It's the poem you have now, Derek."

"Okay . . ." I wanted to hear all this, but I didn't want to, either.

My mother looked closely at me. "Ulysses was there the first time the Rift opened."

I was stunned by her words. "What? *You* know about the Rift between the worlds?"

"All the Longtempses know about it," she said without emotion. "Ulysses was the one who discovered the opening between life and death. He called it the Wound. At the cost of his own life, he found a way to close it. That poem is the story of how Ulysses sent the dead back where they belong."

I nearly dropped to the floor.

"He . . . closed it?" I remembered what Ronny had been trying to say before. Was Ulysses Longtemps the "only person who ever . . ."?

"His young wife buried the poem with him," she went on. "The Longtemps widows after her pledged to keep it secret for as long as it took. The Widows' Pledge."

"For as long as it took?" I said. "For as long as *what* took?"

She turned her eyes to the palely lit windows. "For as long as it took for him to come back," she said simply.

What was she talking about?

"When I saw you had returned to Bayou

Malpierre," she continued, "I knew your journey to find your book had finally begun."

"You mean *his* book," I said. "And I'm not on any kind of journey. Unless you mean a journey away from the crazy dead people who are after me. This is insane —"

The shouting from the floors below was getting louder. Abby? Ronny? Or Erskine Cane?

My mother stepped closer. "You have to close the Wound again."

"What?"

"The evil you saw a hundred and fifty years ago is back. The Wound needs to be closed, just like you did the first time. That's why you're here."

I stared at her, wondering whether she had gone completely nuts over the last ten years. But something she said stirred in me. Bayou Malpierre. I hadn't smelled magnolias only at the cemetery before she abandoned me. I'd smelled them even before that.

At Bayou Malpierre, when I was four.

I had inhaled the scent of magnolias amid the rotting hulks of trees and vines the night I nearly drowned. I'd seen her face, her black hair loose in the water. I remembered it now. It felt like the fog in my head had suddenly cleared.

"You were there in the bayou, weren't you?" I said. "Ten years ago, the night I almost drowned?"

"And finally, we talk about it. Yes, Derek, I was there."

I felt as if hands were twisting my insides. The mystery of my life was going to be solved.

"You saved me that night!" I burst out. "Dad says it wasn't him. Ronny, too. Bonton Fouks didn't see who it was. No one knows anything. But your hair, I remember your hair in the water. And your perfume. It *was* you. You saved me, didn't you, Mom?"

"No, Derek," she said. "I didn't save you."

I saw the black hair coiling about her face in the water. I remembered my mother's fingers reaching for me, grasping my arms under the water.

"But you were there!" I said.

"I was there," she said, her lips trembling. "I saw you."

From the corner of my eye, I saw flames glimmer outside the window. I smelled wood burning, heard the clatter of sticks from the floors below. Abby yelling. Ronny gasping. The two of them calling my name.

"Derek!"

Mom saw the flames, too.

"Time is running out. You have to listen. Ulysses became an officer in the Louisiana Cavalry. He saw death up close, you'll remember it when you read those pages. One day his friend was slain in battle.

Ulysses held him in his arms, watched him die. Then later, he saw him return. Then another returned, and another. Ulysses discovered the Legion. He invented a way to send them back," she said, growing hoarse. "Do you understand? The Legion is growing. They want our world!"

I knew that. I'd been living it.

More glass shattered in the room just below us. Then came a heavy tread on the iron stairs, creaking with the weight.

"You wrote it all, step by step, Ulysses."

"I'm Derek, Mom," I said. "Derek —"

"Forget Derek now," she said firmly. "Ulysses, come out now. Your life depends on it. The Legion knows about you."

"Mom, stop it! Cut it out. You're talking crazy!" I was frozen. I could barely keep myself standing.

"Crazy?" she echoed. "Then how do you know the poem? The words that never left that book?"

"What — I don't — stop it!"

"Ulysses, come out now. Say good-bye to Derek. We have to stop the dead, like you did the first time. But your poem is like a code. Only you can under-stand your words —"

"Stop it!" I screamed. I didn't want to hear it. Couldn't.

She took my shoulders and shook me. "Ulysses, remember the bayou? Remember how you came back from the other side to help us? Remember!"

"Mom! Mom . . ." I wrenched myself free. "I don't care about him or his stupid words that you must have taught me. *You* saved me in the bayou. *You* saved me from drowning."

"I didn't save you. You drowned in the bayou that night."

I clutched her by the arms, pulled myself to her. "No, Mom! You saved me!"

"No, Derek . . . I killed you."

My legs buckled under me. I slipped from her and fell to the floor.

All at once — *foom-foom-foom!* — the walls shook. The door was battered from outside.

My mother pressed something into my hand, a tattered scrap of paper. I wanted to rip it up in front of her, but when I looked up there was only a flutter of curtains, and the whisper of a panel sliding back into place. She was gone.

"Mom? Mom! Don't leave me —"

The door splintered, and Abby tumbled in.

"The house is on fire!" she screamed. Her hands, strong and warm, took mine and pulled me out the door.

⫷ SIXTEEN ⫸

Deader Than Dead

"**C**ane is crazy trying to find you!" Abby said, leading me down the wobbling stairs. "He set the porch on fire, then the parlor —"

I shook my head to clear it. I finally understood who the Legion thought I was. The young captain. Captain Ulysses Perceval Longtemps. No. No. It was all wrong. It couldn't be. But I understood why they hadn't killed me before. They needed me to find the book. Now that I had, everything was simple.

Stop or be stopped.

Kill or be killed.

Cut or be cut.

It was a clear battle, and I was at the center of it. Nothing was by chance. Nothing had ever been by chance. I just didn't know it until now.

Clutching the book, I worked my way with Abby to the main stairs and the entrance hall, near the front doors of the house. Splintered wood was strewn everywhere. One-Arm charged into the room in front of five gray-faced soldiers.

"Surround them," he ordered.

They came at us, and Abby swung her cane so hard that it snapped over the one-armed conductor's head. He dropped to the floor, his head twisted garishly to the side. He shook wildly from waist to neck, a wisp of black fog unfurled from him, and he went still.

Abby screamed to see what she had done. The others paused for a moment, then rushed at us again.

I grabbed Abby's arm and pulled. "Out the back," I said, charging under the stairs. "Where's Ronny?"

"Escaped," she panted. "But I knew you were up there. I had to get you —"

Suddenly the pantry door burst off its hinges. There was Cane himself, torch blazing in his heavy hand. I saw in his eyes, his dead eyes, that he knew who I was, or was supposed to be — the young captain. Ulysses Longtemps.

Cane took a step. Without thinking, I ripped a picture frame off the wall and slammed it at his massive head. He simply held up his free hand and blocked it. The frame shattered. In that second, I ran into Cane's legs.

His feet slid together, sending his giant bulk

tumbling backward, but not before his fingers clawed like daggers across my forehead. They drew blood. I staggered out of the way, but only just. Cane's torch had set the banister ablaze.

"The back door!" Abby dragged me after her. But the back of the house thundered with feet. A troop of dead men swarmed out from under the stairs and pushed us toward the front of the house, which was already crackling with flames.

Waldo was with them. He was pointing at me.

With strength that came from who-knows-where, I swiveled on my heel and knocked blind, creepy little Waldo on his back like a bug. Then I grabbed Abby's hand and, shielding her face, pushed straight through the smoking front doors.

A wall of white flame met us on the other side. We were running so fast that we jumped straight through the fire and onto the steps, tumbling down to the garden.

When I got my bearings, I saw ten or fifteen trucks of all sizes rumbling across the fields with masses of translated souls standing in them. Among the trucks was the fire engine I'd seen before, now crawling with translated dead, some of them the police and firefighters who had come to rescue the living.

There must have been a few hundred Legion soldiers now.

All coming to stop me.

"Holy —" Abby gasped.

The front doors of the house burst open again, and Cane and the others stormed right through the flames at us, howling for blood. My blood.

But there was Ronny, plowing the old black hearse through the rows of marching dead. He roared over to us.

"Get in," he called, spinning out in the garden gravel.

Abby and I jumped into the car. Then Ronny peeled out, careening back through the columns of marching dead. Abby winced. But when I saw the Legion now, no matter how hideous, all I saw were numbers. I saw rows and rows of marching dead that needed to be stopped. Eliminated.

Was that what it meant to be a soldier in this horrible war?

Was I a soldier now?

Without warning, the rear window of the hearse shattered.

"Derek!" Abby gasped. "Behind you —"

Hands pulled me back into the coffin area. Missy Pudge loomed over me, her face gray and blubbery, eyes bulging. Translated. Sounds gargled in her throat, and her fists were like pistons, trying to wrench the book from me. Ronny skidded the hearse toward the stone bridge, picking up speed, while I ripped a curtain rope from the window and twisted it around Missy's gray face. She roared. Then she tore my hands away and threw me against the window. My head snapped on the glass, smashing my bad ear again. I kicked at the back door over and over until it swung wide.

Missy came at me again, but this time Abby thumped her in the face. The woman went flying out the back of the hearse and crumpled onto the dusty road.

"Thanks," I said to Abby, holding my ear. "I needed that."

"You're welcome," she panted. "And yes, you did."

Ronny slowed the hearse. "The Legion's taken the bridge. It's the only way out of here by car."

Through the trees, we could see that the old stone bridge was blocked by three trucks, unloading dozens of dead soldiers. We were cut off from the road on the far side.

Ronny jammed the hearse in reverse, fishtailed, and came to a stop. Masses of the dead were marching across the fields toward us.

We were trapped.

◄| SEVENTEEN |►

The Cavalry

In the moment that followed, I heard the sound of distant hammering — or was it just the blood rushing in my wounded ear? It sounded like battering, thumping, pummeling wildly on iron horseshoes.

"Open the stables," someone said.

Abby turned to me. "What?"

Had *I* said it?

I turned to the misty garden and in my mind I saw the ghost officer and his wife take shape again. Captain Longtemps mounted his horse. But this time he set his face to the darkness and rode off. His call— *"Open the stables!"*

The air flashed to my left. A shriek pierced my ear, a hundred shrieks at once. Out of nowhere, like the storm of wind that threw us off the road earlier, now I saw the stable doors swing open and let loose the snorting and whinnying horses inside. One shape leaped from the mass of crumbled stone, then another and another, hooves clawing air, manes flying, all topped by soldiers in ragged uniforms of butter-nut and gray. It was his cavalry troop from a hundred and fifty years before — Ulysses's troop — their ghostly shapes leaping across the fields in the silver moonlight.

"Take back the bridge . . ." I whispered, and a cry rose up over the fields.

Take back the bridge!

Abby was still staring at me. "Derek? Derek . . ."

The long grass parted in front of the heaving ghost horses as they made for the bridge.

Ronny's eyes were fixed on the bridge. The trucks. The Legion. The screaming horses. "I see them. They're doing it."

"Who?" said Abby.

"Ghosts," said Ronny. "On horses."

"Are you serious?" Abby said. "You can both see them, but I can't? I mean, Ronny, sure. But you, Derek?"

I said nothing.

Like a tornado, the riders crashed across the fields, past the old slave quarters to the old stone bridge, and into the advancing Legion. The voices of the gray-faced dead were wild as they whirled on their feet, fell back. Sabers hacked across the air, sliced the moonlight into slivers of light and dark.

The dead massed closer, but the ghost riders,

though fewer, seemed to outnumber them ten to one. As if commanded, the horsemen swept around the Legion like an eerie and unstoppable storm. I shook. Abby gasped. Ronny murmured under his breath.

"Derek, what happened in that little room?" he asked.

I still said nothing.

Then Cane joined the fight, howling words into the night. The dead turned and moved back over the fields like water receding after a flood. Trucks started up one by one. The Legion retreated.

The bridge was open!

The chorus of shouts from the ghost riders grew louder, filled my ears until I could barely hear the evil dead as the cavalry pushed them across the fields. Away from us.

Away from me.

Soon, all that remained of the scene was what Ulysses never saw — his bride on her knees in the garden, her face in her hands, weeping. Weeping until she was suddenly no longer in white, but dressed head to toe in widows' weeds.

I knew that Ulysses's wife was the first of a long line of widows who pledged to keep his book safe.

Until it was needed. Until now.

Soon even the garden was empty.

Abby looked at me, tears in her eyes.

"Did you see her?" I asked.

She blinked away her tears and shook her head. "No. I was watching you."

I stared and stared as the ghost riders faded away across the fields, following Ulysses's orders.

My orders.

◄| EIGHTEEN |►

The Boy Who . . .

Who was I to say there were no such things as ghosts?

Who was I to say the dead have no power over us?

Who *was* I?

As plumes of smoke filled the air and the red house burned, I told Ronny and Abby what the book was — a long poem, a way to heal the Rift, or the Wound, as I called it now. My mother had told me in the little room.

I told them the poem was written by . . . an ancestor of mine. I couldn't bring myself to say more.

Ronny placed his hand on my arm and spoke in a low voice. "Then we're done here. We have the book. The Legion will be back with a vengeance. But maybe we can find a way to do what Ulysses did. For now, we have to move. Let's go."

"One more thing," I said, wringing my arm free and climbing out of the hearse.

"Derek —" Abby said.

"One more thing!" I repeated, stepping away.

I dug into my pocket, fishing for the paper my mother had given me. I unfolded it slowly and read it by the glow of the burning house.

Dear Derek, it began.

I turned it over and over in my mind — my name of fourteen years. I loved imagining the sound of her voice speaking it.

Dear Derek . . . Dear Derek . . .

I hoped that, in the words that followed, she would take back everything she had told me in the little room. Maybe it was all a test, a dream, a lie.

> *You will hate me for what I have done. But you will see I had no choice. Ulysses was our only hope then, and our only hope now. I gave up my youngest son so that Ulysses could come back — in you — to fight again. Derek, poor little Derek. He died in the bayou that night. He died. Soon you will remember how you went into my little boy.*

I crumpled the letter in rage. "I won't believe it! I won't!" I fell to my knees.

"Derek!" said Abby, climbing out of the hearse and running over to me.

"No!" I stood and moved away from her. From inside my head I heard the reply — cold, clear, and final.

You must believe it.

Suddenly, I was back in the bayou on that night so long ago. I saw my mother's hands in the water above me, not grasping for me as I had thought, and the face of the young man, Ulysses, moving toward me through the water. And I became the water . . . I became . . . him.

Safeguard your book with your life. Lose it, and we lose the war. Decipher it, follow its directions, and the Legion will fall, the Wound will be closed, and life can return. Not for you, but for the others.

Shaking, I looked across the fields and saw only darkness. What was I supposed to do? Would I rot like Ronny? Why could I bleed, when he couldn't? What was the difference between us?

My future was in the past. How did the dead move forward? The answer was in the last paragraph.

I began this letter addressing you by my son's name, Derek Longtemps Stone. I close it by calling you your rightful name.

Go forth, Ulysses Perceval Longtemps. Take up your journey of so many years ago, the voyage only you know — the road of ghosts. The hope of the whole world goes with you.

Your great-granddaughter. Your mother.

Louise Pearline Longtemps

My legs couldn't hold me up. I collapsed to the ground, crushing the letter in my fist. Abby tried to still my shaking hands, but hers were trembling, too.

"What does it say?"

"Let us read it," said Ronny, walking up behind me.

"No," I said. "It's nothing. Nothing." I shoved the letter into my pocket. I couldn't admit it. Not to others. Not to myself. Not yet.

A hot wind shrieked past the burning house, fanning the flames.

Ronny turned to me. "Keep your secret for now. At least you found what the key was hiding before they did. A storm's coming. We'll hide tonight, then decide what to do in the morning. The Legion will be after us in even greater numbers now."

My mother had said the same thing.

The Legion is growing. They want our world!

And Abby's mother — the messenger — had told me, "Find the First. One day only!"

But if I was the captain — if — if I had closed the Wound once before, maybe I could do it again. Maybe I could. Me.

And you?

Do you think this lets you off the hook?

Don't think that just because we held them off this once, you can go back to your iPods and your malls and your cookouts and your normal life.

I can tell you right now, this war won't let you.

The Legion won't let you.

So what should you do?

Run.

Another hot wind swept past. Amaranthia, the great red house, had waited a hundred and fifty years for Ulysses Perceval Longtemps to return. Now it shuddered and quivered and finally collapsed on itself.

Amaranthia. Lost again.

I thought back to that morning, only nine hours before. If I believed what my mother had told me, it was now so far in the past it meant nothing.

That was the past of Derek Stone.

The boy who died.

"Ronny's right," said Abby, tugging my arm gently.

"My mother's out there somewhere. Maybe she'll help us again. There's nothing for us here. We have to go. Our job's not done yet."

It hurt to see Abby becoming a soldier, too. Like Ronny. And like me.

Some army we had.

Maybe we stood a chance.

With a last look at the burning wreckage, I climbed back into the hearse, turning toward the voyage only I knew — the road of ghosts.

Ronny started the engine, threw the old hearse in gear, and we raced off into the gathering night.

Don't miss the next volume in Derek's story . . .

The Ghost Road

Turn the page for a special sneak peek!

THE GHOST ROAD

After I finished throwing up, we started driving again.

My brother, Ronny, and Abby Donner were silent as we tore up the foggy roads outside Coushatta in a huge old hearse. It was the third time I had gotten sick in as many hours. They were getting tired of it.

"Sorry," I mumbled. But I wasn't. Throwing up was my body's way of saying, "Nope. Can't digest this insanity. No way."

You'd chuck it all up too if, right out of the blue, someone told you — no, if hundreds of people told you —

"You hear that?" Abby interrupted my thoughts.

Ronny took his eyes from the review mirror and slowed the car. "What?"

"Shhh." She craned her neck around to the back window. "I thought I heard . . ."

Ronny pulled over to the shoulder near a stretch of weedy, broken fence and flicked off the headlights. "I don't hear —"

Abby screamed. "A truck!"

Wrong. Three trucks, racing out of the fog behind us.

Ronny jammed his foot on the gas and spun the wheel. The hearse slid behind the fence, throwing Abby and me to the floor. Ronny jerked to a stop and shut off the motor, just as one, two, three trucks shot past us, racing north toward Shreveport.

I couldn't see the faces of the drivers, but I could hear their voices — whining, angry, squealing, groaning. I knew those drivers.

They were dead.

The trucks didn't slow down. We had escaped. For now.

Ronny snorted to himself. "Well, that could've been bad."

Abby gave him a swat with the road map. It wasn't playful. "Why can't you just drive like a normal person?"

Ronny turned to her, his face suddenly cold. "You want reasons?"

That was a joke. Sort of.

Ronny wasn't a normal person. He was dead.

It probably explains why he's not a good driver. But with the Legion after you, bad driving isn't such a big deal.

The Legion?

Man, I hope you've been listening to what I've already told you, because there's no time now for a big story.

Today is when it all happens.

Ronny skidded the car — a beat-up 1954 Cadillac hearse about a block and a half long — back onto the road, and we drove on.

"Ronny, will you slow down!" said Abby almost immediately.

"Uh, no," he said. "It'll be dawn in an hour. And I'm pretty sure it was your dead mom who said —"

"Don't talk about her like that!" Abby shouted.

"Stuff it, and find a road map," Ronny replied.

Yeah. They weren't getting along. Ronny was on edge like nobody's business, and I knew part of the reason. He had a patch of dead flesh on his neck and chin. It had been growing by the hour.

Erskine Cane's low growling coiled deeply in my

ear, like a snake boring into my brain. I knew he was twenty minutes away, no more.

But the voices of the dead weren't the only things crowding my brain.

"Will you hurry up and read that thing?" Ronny snapped, glancing at me. "We don't have forever."

"Cut Derek some slack, will you?" said Abby.

"Just read that thing!"

"That thing" was *The Ghost Road*, a fifty-page poem sitting in my lap. It was scribbled in scratchy black ink during the Civil War by a young captain named Ulysses Longtemps.

He's . . . an ancestor of mine.

The poem describes how Ulysses witnessed the first translation ever, during Louisiana's Red River campaign in 1864. It tells how Ulysses discovered the Wound between our worlds, and how he eventually closed it and sent the dead back to the afterlife.

All that happened a hundred and forty five years ago.

Of course, *The Ghost Road* was written in a kind of code, and apparently I was the only one who could understand it.

A code and a poem. Two big strikes against it.

Or maybe three.

Besides the weird, flowery language of the poem, odd doodles, bizarre sketches, and equations were scribbled in the margins. I remembered some of them from seventh grade geometry, but some I'd never seen before.

Whatever *The Ghost Road* was, the Legion wanted it. They wanted me, sure. But they also wanted that book.

We came to a crossroads, and Ronny slowed the hearse.

A lone stop sign was stuck in the ground, tilted severely away from the road, as if someone had rolled over it.

Ronny snickered, incredulous. "Now what?"

We were trying to find the First, and the book was our guide. That, and a map Abby had dug out of the hearse's ancient glove compartment.

"Can you read the words to us again?" Abby asked me, scanning the map by the dim dashboard light.

It was dark in the car, but I managed to find the lines that seemed to describe the place we were looking for:

The river bends like weeping willow limbs
And there I thought I saw a widow bend to her dead
    love,
And saw his body bending in the tangled swamp.

"Lot of bending going on," said Ronny coolly.

I didn't read them the next line, though I couldn't get it out of my mind.

By end of day, I knew, that dead love may be me.

"Wait," said Abby, tracing her finger across the map. "There's a place called Cemetery Bend coming up in a few miles. It's on the river, and there's a cross marked here. Do you think —"

"Sounds like the place," Ronny said. The engine growled as he raced off again, burning rubber.

Abby sulked. "You waste gas every time you do that —"

"So do you, when you open your mouth," Ronny muttered.

"Well, at least *I'm* not decaying," Abby said.

"Shut up!" I cried. "And pull over!"

Ronny braked fast, and I lurched out of the car, feeling my stomach flip over again. But it wasn't their arguing that was making me sick.

In Ulysses Longtemps's old room at Amaranthia, among a chorus of weeping widows and the smell of magnolia, my mother had told me the most terrible secret of all.

Leaning away from the hearse, spilling what was left of my guts on the ground, I remembered what she told me, and wondered what kind of hearse had carried me when I died.

When I died.

If I actually believed what my mother told me, I didn't *nearly* drown in that filthy bayou when I was four. I just plain drowned.

Not only that, but at the instant I drowned, I was reanimated by the soul of that old poet captain, Ulysses Longtemps. The world needed him more than me. After all, he had closed the Wound.

In other words, since I was four I haven't been quite myself. I've been him.

It's like:

Hi, I'm Derek Stone. I've been dead most of my life.

Or:

Hi, I'm Derek. My next birthday is a hundred and fifty years ago.

You can't imagine the mess in my head right now. Derek Stone. Ulysses Longtemps. Old ghosts. The evil Legion.

Everyone trying to get a word in.

Abby didn't know about it yet. Poor Abby — just a nice girl holding a cheesecake when I first saw her on that train. It seemed like a few hundred lifetimes ago. Ronny didn't know who I really was, either, but I wondered how long it would take him to guess. I hadn't figured out how to tell them. I hardly believed it myself.

Except that I was kind of forced to.

Trees flashed by. Abby murmured something about the map. Ronny muttered behind the wheel, searching, always searching.

I knew it was up to me to find Cemetery Bend and the Wound between this world and the next. However Ulysses managed to close it, I had to find out in the next few hours. Otherwise, the First would open the Wound even more, and our world would be over-run with thousands — millions! — of dead souls.

. . . dark souls will flood the darkened earth from every
  drop of dark water . . .

Lots of darkness going on.

"I thought you guys could hear the dead," said Abby, glancing in the rearview mirror just then. "Because, believe it or not, we have company."

I swiveled in my seat and looked back at the curv-ing road.

Headlights glowed in the fog behind us. I counted four pairs of lights, but there were more. I'd been so wrapped up in my own mind, I hadn't heard the dead. But Ronny hadn't heard them, either. Why not?

"Lose them," I said.

Tires screeched as Ronny slid the car around a corner, bumping the guardrail three times. Then I heard a police siren. A cruiser tore out from a side road. A police motorcycle was right behind him. The tinny loudspeaker demanded that we all pull over.

Ronny sped up.

If the Legion were smart, or if they cared, they would have split up and gone on their way. But they weren't smart. They were deadly. And the only things they cared about were getting that book, and getting rid of me.

Whoever I was.

THE SCARIEST

PLACE ON EARTH!

Discover the world on the other side of night...
Meet

OLIVER NOCTURNE

He's not your typical vampire.

#1: THE VAMPIRE'S PHOTOGRAPH

#2: THE SUNLIGHT SLAYINGS

#3: BLOOD TIES

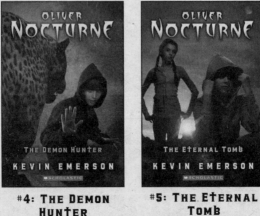

#4: THE DEMON HUNTER

#5: THE ETERNAL TOMB